BLACK SOLDIER

Doubleday Signal Books

BONNIE

PONY OF THE SIOUX

THE JUNGLE SECRET

NORTH POLE: THE STORY OF
ROBERT PEARY

BASEBALL BONUS KID

CAROL HEISS: OLYMPIC QUEEN

GREEN LIGHT FOR SANDY

SEA TREASURE

THE BLOOD RED BELT

KENDALL OF THE COAST GUARD

RODEO ROUNDUP

NANCY KIMBALL, NURSE'S AIDE

FOOTBALL FURY

CIVIL WAR SAILOR

DINNY AND DREAMDUST

AUSTIN OF THE AIR FORCE

THE LONG REACH

FOOTLIGHTS FOR JEAN

BASEBALL SPARK PLUG

RUNAWAY TEEN

LIGHTNING ON ICE

HOT ROD THUNDER

JUDY NORTH, DRUM MAJORETTE

DIRT TRACK DANGER

ADVENTURE IN ALASKA

CLIMB TO THE TOP

FISHING FLEET BOY

JACK WADE, FIGHTER FOR LIBERTY

THE MYSTERY OF HIDDEN HARBOR

SCANLON OF THE SUB SERVICE

A SUMMER TO REMEMBER

NAT DUNLAP, JUNIOR "MEDIC"

BLAST-OFF! A TEEN ROCKET
ADVENTURE

TWO GIRLS IN NEW YORK

THE MYSTERY OF THE FLOODED
MINE

CATHY AND LISETTE

EVANS OF THE ARMY

HIGH SCHOOL DROP OUT

DOUBLE TROUBLE

PRO FOOTBALL ROOKIE

THE MYSTERY OF BLUE STAR
LODGE

ADVENTURE IN DEEPMORE CAVE

FAST BALL PITCHER

HI PACKETT, JUMPING CENTER

NURSE IN TRAINING

SHY GIRL: THE STORY OF
ELEANOR ROOSEVELT

SKI PATROL

BIG BAND

GINNY HARRIS ON STAGE

GRACIE

THREE CHEERS FOR POLLY

SECOND YEAR NURSE

FEAR RIDES HIGH

THE MYSTERY OF THE INSIDE
ROOM

ARTHUR ASHE: TENNIS CHAMPION

THE MYSTERY OF THE THIRD-HAND
SHOP

GOING, GOING, GONE

THE KID FROM CUBA: ZOILO
VERSALLES

GANG GIRL

TV DANCER

ROAR OF ENGINES

DONNA DEVARONA: GOLD MEDAL
SWIMMER

PETE CASS: SCRAMBLER

BLACK SOLDIER

QUEEN OF ENGLAND: THE STORY
OF ELIZABETH I

TROUBLE AT MERCY HOSPITAL

TRAPPED IN SPACE

THE GHOSTS OF LEE HOUSE

BLACK SOLDIER

by John Clarke

Illustrated by Harold James

DOUBLEDAY & COMPANY, INC.
Garden City, New York

LIBRARY OF CONGRESS CATALOG CARD NUMBER 68–17808
COPYRIGHT © 1968 BY DOUBLEDAY & COMPANY, INC.
ALL RIGHTS RESERVED
PRINTED IN THE UNITED STATES OF AMERICA
PREPARED BY RUTLEDGE BOOKS
FIRST EDITION

Contents

CHAPTER 1

"Ever Been South?"

He was going to war!

George Bunty was signed up. He was going to be in uniform, a GI, fighting in World War II. Would he be sent to the Pacific to fight the Japanese? Or would he be shipped across the Atlantic to fight the Germans? It did not matter. All he wanted was to get into action.

It was July, 1943. Outside the train window, the sun beat down. The cars were hot, filled with young men, sweating, talking—all of them headed for Camp Ashton.

The boy next to Bunty grinned hello. "Where you from?" he shouted above the noise.

"Woodside," Bunty yelled back. "You?"

"Brooklyn, U.S.A. My name is Luzzi. We ought to hit camp pretty soon, right?"

"Just coming in!" Bunty yelled. "Man, here we are!"

The train jerked to a stop. Doors opened. Young men

of all sizes and shapes jumped out. A U. S. Army officer hurried past and climbed up on a platform. Two sergeants rushed up to get the loud speaker into operation. Suddenly the voice of the officer boomed out:

"You men will move out of here by truck. Men on the north side of me load into trucks over here. Men on the south load into trucks on this side. When a truck is filled, move on to the next one. Okay, move out!"

MPs—the Army's military policemen—white belts around their waists and white bands on their helmets, herded the men in the right direction. Bunty, with Luzzi at his side, spotted the trucks, the big six-wheel rack jobs. A short Negro with big ears and a broad grin ran up to Bunty. "Take a bet?" he said eagerly. "Two bits we get in the fifth truck. Hey, man, take a bet with Meeps!"

"Knock it off, soldier!" an MP yelled, and Meeps ducked in between Bunty and Luzzi.

"Whooo-eee!" he said under his breath. "Those boys got ears in the backs of their heads! Give you two bits we hit the fifth truck."

Nobody took his bet. The MPs urged them up over the tail gates of the trucks. When one truck was filled, the rest of the men went on to the next one. Tail gates slammed shut. Engines roared. The smell of burning gas and oil filled the air, and the trucks rolled out onto the road to the camp.

"Ten coconuts to one palm tree we draw the Pacific," Meeps offered quickly, and everyone laughed.

The trucks lumbered through the entrance gates of the fort and along the main camp road. They passed row after row of two-story buildings, all alike. Here and there, signs marked one group of buildings or another as belonging to the 386th Engineers, or some other outfit, and Bunty thought of belonging to one of them. A general's car sped past. A breeze caught at the flag raised above the parade grounds and sent it streaming against the bright blue sky.

Bunty's stomach muscles grew tight. It was the same feeling he had known when he first applied for a job after he graduated from high school—pride and excitement, and a little bit of worry. Not much worry, though. He had done well in high school. He didn't have to be ashamed of his record.

An ad in the paper had said a company offered to train 25 high school graduates for "high-paying positions." He had phoned the number and been told to come in for an interview. There were quite a few other people being interviewed that day, among them a boy named Johnson —a white boy—Bunty had known at high school.

Johnson went in first. When he came out, he was grinning. "Got it!" he told Bunty, making a circle with thumb and finger.

Johnson had been a big goof-off in school. If he could make the grade, Bunty surely could.

But when Bunty went in, the man who interviewed him asked him hardly any questions at all. He just said, "Sorry, we have nothing for you at this time."

There was only one way to figure it, Bunty knew, as he walked home. If they took a goof-off like Johnson and didn't take a good student like George Bunty, it was because Johnson was white and Bunty was black.

But now, Bunty told himself with satisfaction, things would be different. The Army was part of the United States Government. There would be no difference between white and black in the Army.

Sergeants got out of the truck cabs and opened the tail gates. Bunty and the others jumped down.

"Line up! Line up! Come on, make a line now!"

Short and tall, fat and thin, they lined up in the hot sun. The line began to move forward slowly.

"We ever going to get there?" Meeps demanded. "I hope they give me an M-1."

"What you'll get is a needle," a big boy muttered.

Meeps threw up his hands in mock fear, and Luzzi laughed. He pulled a package of gum from his pocket and gave Bunty a stick, and then Meeps and the big boy. The good feeling in Bunty swelled.

The line moved into a building. Raw beams angled over their heads. Bare wooden counters stretched the length of the room, and behind them were shelves as high as a man could reach. Soldiers in fatigues—green work uniforms—stood behind the counters. The first one handed each man two laundry bags, one blue and one tan.

"What size shoes, soldier?" the next man asked.

"Twelve," Bunty said.

Two pairs of high work shoes were dumped on the counter. "Put them in your A bag," the soldier ordered, and when Bunty hesitated, he barked: "The blue bag— the blue bag!"

The line inched forward. Bunty collected the rest of his clothing—shirts and pants, green work fatigues, underwear, four pairs of socks, and the rest of his clothes, stuffing them into the A and B bags as directed. He was motioned to the far side of the building with the others. Meeps grinned up at Bunty.

"Hey, man, you got your bags mixed up."

"How come?" Bunty asked.

"You are carrying your A bag in your B hand, and your B bag in your A hand," Meeps declared. For a minute Bunty's face went blank, and then he understood that it was a joke and laughed with the others.

The captain who had been at the train station walked in. A sergeant barked for silence. The captain shot a business-like look at the men. "As your name is called, step across to the counter. Take your laundry bags with you." He began to call out names: "*Abel . . . Anderson . . . Barnes. . . .*"

The men moved across the floor. Bunty's name was

called and he joined the new line. The list of names went on: *"Loomis . . . Lumpton . . . Meeps. . . ."*

It hit Bunty suddenly, like a fist in the stomach. All the men being called were Negroes. No white men's names were read out, no Negroes were skipped. Bunty felt a new silence in the room as others realized what was happening. He glanced down his line. Meeps was standing very still, the grin gone from his face. Bunty looked across to the white line and his eyes met Luzzi's. Luzzi looked away.

The captain finished the list and walked out. The sergeant boomed at them: "All right, you GIs, saddle up and move out."

Shouldering their bags, they went from the building into the hot sun and headed down a road away from the main camp. The sergeant urged them along.

"Let's make it look like something! Get in step there. Left, right, left . . . *Hut, hup, hip, haw. . . .*"

They marched for what seemed to Bunty about five city blocks, then turned right past the last of the wooden buildings, crossed a road, and came to a tent city. Rows of tents—big ones set on wooden floors—stretched along the streets. The sergeant pulled them to a halt.

"Here are your homes away from home for a couple of days," he told them. "When you go in the door, the first man takes the first bunk, the second man the next, and so on. No fighting over bunks. If you want to change later, you can. But peaceful! You hear?"

Some of the men bent to pick up their packs. *"Ten-hut!"* The sergeant bellowed. "In this man's army, don't make a move until you are ordered. Count off by twenties. First twenty in the first tent, next twenty in the next, and so on. Let's hear it!"

They counted off. "Okay, now," the sergeant yelled. "Nice and quiet. Pile your stuff on the bunks for now. Take off your clothes—down to your skin—and put them in a bundle to send home. Get into your fatigues, and be ready to fall out in 15 minutes!"

Bunty went into the first tent. The place was in confusion as men claimed bunks and dug into their bags, trying to find the right clothes. Bunty had just started to strip down when Meeps popped up at his side.

"How did you get in here?" Bunty demanded.

Meeps' grin stretched wide. "Sergeant said we could trade. So that's what I did, man!"

"From one tent to another?"

"He never mentioned tents. I just skinned back and talked a good trade."

Outside the sergeant bellowed: "Seven minutes!" Meeps got into his army shorts and howled. They were the wrong size. He hopped about, clutching them to him.

"Nobody got a pin, how am I going to keep my drawers up?"

"Pull your pants up over them. Maybe they'll stay," Bunty laughed, and Meeps obeyed, looking unhappy.

"Fall out! Fall out!" the sergeant shouted.

"That's what I'm going to do," Meeps muttered, clapping his fatigue hat on to his head.

They lined up. The sergeant pulled them to attention and marched up and down looking them over.

"Real spit and polish," he said. "Yes sir, real polish." He laughed at his own joke. "Okay, you sad sacks, let's straighten up that line."

They began, that minute, to be soldiers. Chests came out, stomachs came in. The sergeant took in every detail.

"Lace up those boots, soldier. . . . Button that button. . . . Get that sleeve straight. . . ."

In two days they were slapped into rough shape. They could line up straight, tallest man to the right. They could hold a marching column that wasn't too crooked. They could come to attention and salute with a snap.

They were even beginning to tell time army style. George Bunty now recognized that 0900 hours meant nine o'clock in the morning, that 1200 hours was noon, that 1800 hours was six o'clock in the evening.

Their orders for basic training came on the third morning right after chow. Each company lined up and came to attention as a staff sergeant walked up.

"At ease," he barked. "The following men will turn in their bedding and foot lockers, and fall out at 0900 with all other gear in bags. Wear your Class A uniforms."

A stir went through the ranks. They knew what this meant. Some of them were moving out to permanent camps to start basic. Hopefully, they would leave the tents. Once fight training began, maybe color would be forgotten. Excitement went down Bunty's spine. He wanted to get going.

His name was called. A huge grin split his face, and he punched the air with a fast one-two. The guy next to him gave him a look of envy. His name started with A and he had been passed over. Meeps was another name called.

They rushed to their tent. "Where we going, man?" Meeps demanded.

"Who knows?" Bunty said, stuffing gear into his bag. "But at least we are on our way."

"Wish it was Berlin!" Meeps said.

"Me too," Bunty answered.

By 0900 those who had been called were milling eagerly in the hot sun, waiting for orders. A ripple of pride went through Bunty. They looked good in their Class A's, shoes gleaming with polish, buckles shining in the sun. The same question was on every man's lips: "Where do you think we are headed?"

They snapped through roll call. Trucks lumbered up, and they climbed in. They went down the main camp road, cheering and yelling. At the station, a troop train was pulled up. Tossing their bags up the steps, they got aboard.

Then they were moving, back along the way they had come, to Penn Station in New York City. There was no getting out of the cars here. They were hauled back and forth on the tracks, getting into position. An hour passed, and nothing happened.

"Man, the war's going to be over before we get out of here," Meeps muttered.

"You know how they do it in the Army." Bunty grinned. "Hurry up and wait."

It was four o'clock before they got going, and a cheer went up when they came out into daylight. The men peered out the windows. Gray factory walls gave way to the flat open spaces of swamp land.

"New Jersey," Bunty said, watching the green meadows pass. When he was a kid, he had hunted rabbits near here with his dad on Sundays. He thought of home, the narrow house set close to other houses just like it, neat patches of yard in front and in back. His dad had a talent for making things grow. Every summer night when he got home from his job at the post office, he worked in the yard until Mom called him to supper.

Bunty remembered when he had first told them he was trying to get into the Army . . . the pride in his dad's face, the pride mixed with fear in his mother's. And he remembered how hard it had been getting in, because when a draft call had come to his area, it hadn't been for 100 men, or 124. It had been for 120 whites and 4 Negroes. But Bunty had made it. And his mom had cried when he came rushing home with the news. The night before he left, she had cooked him his favorite dinner.

The thought of food made Bunty realize how hungry he was. He stretched his neck, looking toward the front of the car, just as a sergeant pushed through the door.

"Break out your mess kits!" he bawled. "Chow car up ahead."

There was a happy shout and a scramble for mess kits. They swayed through the car ahead, trading jokes with the men they passed. Chow was stew, but it tasted good. A tall, good-looking boy with a serious face spoke to Bunty. "Where do you think we are headed?"

"South," Bunty said.

"Ever been South?" the boy asked. Bunty shook his head. "Me neither. Name is Cranston—Ned Cranston, from Syracuse, New York. I was in college there—second year." He was silent a moment. "I'll finish when I get back."

And Bunty nodded.

Darkness gathered outside the train. Lights flashed past them now and then. Men were getting ready for bed, tired and ready to hit the sack. The car Bunty was in became quiet and, in the quiet, he could feel doubts beginning to form and spread slowly out like a fog creeping in from the ocean.

CHAPTER 2

"I Won't Take That!"

The train ride took them five days—five days of sitting on side tracks, waiting for freight and passenger trains to pass, being taken off one train and coupled to another.

"If we ever get where we are going, I'm not going to get on another train as long as I live," Meeps vowed. "Whooo-eee! Look at that rain!"

It was still raining when, late that afternoon of the fifth day, they bumped to their last stop and spilled out onto an ancient, wooden station platform that seemed to be the jumping-off place to nowhere. The open backs of trucks with flapping canvas covers waited for them. Grunting and swearing, they tossed their gear aboard.

"Where are we?" Meeps complained loudly.

"Camp Rushmore, Alabama," an MP shouted, slamming the tail gate shut.

They bounced over a rough road, rumbled down a

stretch of highway, turned between the stone pillars of an entrance where guards stood on duty. They glimpsed the camp through the rain, branched off the main camp road and came, at last, to their barracks—a row of low, garage-like buildings.

A sergeant hupped them in—and it was Camp Ashton again without tents.

The roll was called, they were assigned bunks, chewed out, and chowed down with snap-to-it speed. They felt the change of pace, all of them. Regular life was gone. This was all Army.

They walked through the rain to the supply room where they were loaded with gear: gas mask, helmet, canteen for holding water, bedding, pack, first-aid kit, bayonet. And their M-1 rifles. The smooth wood of the stock felt good in Bunty's hands.

"Hey, man," he thought. "Private Bunty, reporting for duty!"

"Back to your barracks!" the sergeant ordered, and they marched back, trying to hold on to everything, feeling the mud sticking to their boots.

If they had hoped for bed, they were out of luck. They spent an hour struggling to learn how to make up their bunks. Bunty cornered his sheets without any trouble. His mother had been a nurse, and she had always been particular about the way he made his bed.

He finished ahead of the others, saw Ned Cranston struggling, and made the V-for-Victory sign.

Sergeant Morrison stopped beside his bunk and gave his work a pitying look. "Stretch those blankets, soldier!" he ordered. "In the Army they have to be tight enough so a dime will bounce on them."

Bunty's face fell, and he set to work to do his bed over.

"Whooo-eee!" Meeps said under his breath. "I'm going to sleep on the floor, if I ever get this thing made right."

At last the sergeant was satisfied. But they were not through yet. He picked up Bunty's rifle and held it up.

"This is a rifle," he said. "Never call it a gun. And don't drop it. This is your best friend. After tomorrow, you carry it with you wherever you go. Got that?"

"Yes, sir," the men answered.

"Okay," Sergeant Morrison said. "Now before lights out, learn your rifle number—and remember it! Okay, hop to it!"

Men sat on the floor and on foot lockers, already learning that bunks were not to sit on unless you wanted to get caught with blankets wrinkled at a surprise inspection. Meeps frowned as he tried to remember his rifle number. Bunty recited his over and over, and then wrote them on a piece of paper, which he tucked into his blouse pocket.

Fifteen minutes later the rifles were collected and locked in the racks. The men crawled into their bunks. It seemed to Bunty that he had hardly closed his eyes when a whistle blasted him awake, and Sergeant Morrison was shouting: "Rise and shine! Rise and shine! Fall out in the company street in fifteen minutes wearing fatigues."

There was a rush for the wash rooms. Men bumped each other, trying to get a chance at the wash bowls. The first day had begun, and from then on they worked, sweated, drilled, studied, crawled in the dust, hit the dirt, marched in mud, listened to lectures, and learned to salute anything that moved.

It was rough and it was tough. "Okay, you men! You are members of the 309th Engineer Training Battalion. So measure up now!" And they did. It was their outfit, and it was going to be good.

"Maybe we didn't make the Infantry the way a lot of us wanted," Bunty wrote home, "but there's nothing soft about the Engineers. It's a great outfit."

He didn't write about the bad part. Why send his folks bad news when there was nothing to be done about it? He did not tell about the closed-off area for Negroes out on the edge of camp. Or about the separate mess hall. Or the second-class store and recreation center. He did not write about their CO—the commanding officer—who had been appointed to his post because, as a southern white officer, he "knew how to handle the Blacks."

Bunty felt all of these things. They hit him hard, as they did all the men. But he put disappointment behind him. He wondered, had he really expected things to be different in the Army? Maybe all he had done was hope —hope that in fighting for his country they might be.

He knew one thing. He was going to do well. They all were. And if they did, it would prove that they were good soldiers—and good men.

And they were good. In a very short time they could out march, out drill any company on the base. When Sergeant Morrison put them through their paces, no unit could beat them. And Sergeant Morrison grinned happily. He liked these men, and he was proud of them.

One morning they were ordered out to the gas field. Masks hooked to their belts, instructions fresh in their minds, they marched to a large shed standing away from all the buildings. An ambulance waited beside it.

Sergeant Morrison lined them up. "You are going into the barn," he told them. "If you did not learn anything from the lecture and the movie, you'll be gassed."

Men looked at each other. They counted off. Bunty marched into the building with the first group. It smelled funny. Bunty's throat felt tight.

"Keep your hands off your masks!" the sergeant barked. "Don't touch them until the order is given!"

Bunty stood still. The gas smell was stronger now. In the back of the room, a soldier began to moan and was taken out.

"*Gas!*" a sergeant yelled, trying to make them use their masks before the order was given. It took nerve to stand there, to keep hands away from masks. Nobody moved.

Then the order came. "Masks on!" In a split second, Bunty had his in place. He was afraid to breathe at first, not sure he could trust the mask. But then he was trying it, soft and easy. A feeling of relief went through him when he found that it worked.

The officer let them stand there until each man had learned for himself that the masks could be trusted. Then he marched them out, and the next group went in.

Only three men had to be taken out. Only one tried to run out. Morrison marched them back to the barracks, looking pleased.

"Okay," he said. "GI party tonight. Everybody back in the barracks right after chow."

The men were excited. "Music, maybe . . . Think there'll be girls? . . . We get to wear our Class A's?"

But the order of the day was fatigues—their work clothes. Instead of girls, there were mops and buckets. Instead of music, scrubbing floors.

"So that's a GI party," Meeps groaned. "Man, I'd have bet most anything it was for real."

A week later they had their toughest day yet: body rolling away from tanks. After watching a training movie, they marched to the tank field, and spread out on order.

"Okay—*hit the dirt!*" Morrison bellowed. "*Now roll!*"

Bunty hit the dirt. Dust flew up. His canteen dug into him as he rolled. His elbow hit a rock.

"Move those bodies!" the sergeant yelled. "Come on, move it."

Over and over again they aimed their rifles as though firing at a tank, threw themselves on the ground, and rolled. The sun beat down on them. Sweat made rivers of mud through the dust on Bunty's face.

A whistle sounded. Over the hill came four soldiers in a jeep, yelling: *"Tanks!"*

And then the tanks came, playing the role of German panzer tanks. Sergeants stood with their heads out of the openings in the tank tops. Dust rose in a thick cloud over the field. Above the noise a sergeant called: "Do not run when attacked! Fire at the gun barrels!"

Bunty saw a tank coming in. He wheeled, dry-fired, and hit the dirt. The tank turned away, taking after someone else, and a second tank bore down on Bunty.

"Roll, nigger, or I'll crease your black hide!" The shout came from inside the tank—from the red-faced sergeant whose head Bunty had seen out of the tank as it came over the hill.

Rage shot through Bunty. He was on his feet, one thought in mind: to haul the man out of the tank and drive a fist into his face.

Ned Cranston had heard the shout, and he knew what was going to happen. He rolled himself into Bunty, grabbing his legs, knocking him down. Bunty tried to get free, but Cranston pinned him to the ground.

"Knock it off!" he said hoarsely.

"Get off me!" Bunty choked. "I won't take that!"

Cranston shoved his face close to Bunty's. "He *wants* you to make a move! Try to fight him, and the Army will throw the book at you. Don't play into his hands, man! Don't give him what he wants!"

Through the dust, Bunty could see the face of the tank sergeant, and in it he saw the waiting and hoping. He got to his feet. The challenge in his eyes was clear and hard. The sergeant's look turned ugly.

Then the duel began. The tank came at Bunty. Bunty aimed and rolled, and the tank was almost on him. He didn't move a muscle. The tank backed off, and Bunty sprang to position. And the tank was at him again. Bunty held his place until the last second, and then dry-fired and rolled. The tank rumbled past.

The sergeant shouted orders to turn and attack, but Bunty was ready. Again he waited until the last second, and then rolled away. It went on for the rest of the hour. Once the sergeant got him, and Bunty saw the tank tracks moving in on him. He sucked in his breath, sure that those tracks were going to crush him into the ground. But he wouldn't move, and the tank stopped, its tracks touching his body.

At last the whistle brought the exercise to a halt, pulling the tanks out. Bunty got to his feet, sweat and

dirt soaking his blouse. He watched the tanks go off the field knowing he had won.

As they fell in, he caught Cranston's look of triumph, and behind him he heard Meeps say softly: "That was sweet. Real sweet. That sarge, he's the most unhappy man in this whole camp right now. He sure thought he could bust you."

But nothing could—Bunty was ready to swear it.

CHAPTER 3

"Where You Going, Boy?"

Now they were into the last two weeks of Basic. The weather was hot, and they sweated it out. They began to count the days: three more, two. And then it was the final Thursday. Tomorrow they would have passes to town—the first any man had had in thirteen long weeks.

"Man, I'm going to eat three quarts of ice cream," Meeps declared. "You want to bet two-bits I can?"

"You'd win, all right." Bunty laughed. He stretched out on his bunk, hands behind his head. "What I want," he said, "is a steak. A big, rare steak. I can see it now—two inches thick and dripping juice."

"You'd better put it out of your head for now," Ned Cranston said with a grin. "It's time for chow, and you know what that means."

"Turnip greens and boiled mutton."

"How come there's nothing but mutton and pork in

this man's army?" Meeps piped up. "I eat so much of them I squeal like a pig or baa like a sheep every time I hear mess call."

"Don't you know?" Cranston teased. "Those are the CO's 'Black Boy Specials.' He orders them straight from Washington, D.C.—he knows what us Negroes want."

There was a howl of laughter, and Meeps walked up and down the aisle mimicking the CO. But Bunty noticed that Loftus, a tall, thin Negro with a scar on his right cheek, and a few of the others weren't laughing. It hit him suddenly: he had never seen Loftus laugh.

The barracks were full of activity that afternoon. Boots and brass were polished, every piece of equipment checked out. Bunty took the cup off his canteen and cleaned the inside of it.

At 1600 they fell in for full dress parade. Rifle barrels shone in the sun. Trousers were creased knife sharp. A wave of pride went through Bunty. They looked smart and snappy, and they pulled to attention sharply at the command. Captain Tarbell, his uniform perfectly cut, marched down the ranks.

He stopped in front of Bunty, who presented arms. "Name, rank, and number," the captain barked.

"Private George Bunty, 32154185, sir," Bunty snapped out, remembering to keep his eyes on the top button of the captain's blouse as orders required.

The captain marched on. Meeps was called out and inspection of his canteen demanded. The whole com-

31

pany breathed a sigh of relief. He had remembered to clean the inside of the cup.

Captain Tarbell stepped out in front of them. "You men are now soldiers in the United States Army," he said. "This is a great honor for you. See that you maintain the honor of the uniforms you wear. You will have passes to town. See that you remember your place, and don't let me hear any bad reports."

Bunty's back stiffened. He sensed the sudden tight feeling among the ranks. He knew that every man hated the words: 'Remember your place.' The captain marched away, and the men were dismissed.

They moved forward in a line. In spite of the captain's words, there was great excitement. Sergeant Morrison called out the names, one after another. When Bunty's name came he stepped forward and grasped the slip of white paper handed to him. "Private George Bunty," it read. "32154185 . . . B Company . . . Engineers . . . signed: Captain Orville B. Tarbell."

Half an hour later they were piling into the waiting busses. Laughing and singing, they rode into town and spilled out at the station. Soldiers took off, alone and in groups, all eager for a good time.

Bunty walked along the main street of the town. It was not a big town, but the store windows were bright, and the people on the streets were not army. He hadn't realized how much he had missed home life.

Up ahead he saw a big red, white, and blue sign:

USO. That was a good place to start his leave, he thought. He could find out about places to go, maybe have some coffee and doughnuts.

He crossed the street to the USO entrance and started in. A policeman stopped him.

"Where you going, boy?"

"The USO," Bunty said, trying to shut his mind to the word, 'boy.'

The policeman shook his head. "You aren't going in there," he said. He flipped his thumb at a sign over the door. Bunty looked at it, and the two words seemed to jump out at him: WHITE ONLY.

It was the first time he had ever seen those words printed on a sign. He had read about them, but he had never seen them before. He stood staring at them, a cold spot growing in the middle of his stomach.

"Move on," the policeman said, and pushed him with his club.

Bunty turned and stared at the policeman. He saw in the man's face no expression, only the accepting of rules, and Bunty knew he would use his club.

Bunty walked on down the street. He passed a sign that said: *Uncle Sam Needs You . . . Fight for Freedom* And in his mind, the two words on that other sign seemed to flash in bright lights: WHITE ONLY . . . WHITE ONLY. . . .

A man and woman came out of a *café*, laughing and talking. The woman had on a beaded green dress and

long, fancy earrings. She turned back to plant a kiss on the fat man's cheek, and she wasn't watching where she was going. She stumbled on the *café* step and fell into Bunty. Bunty put out his hand to stop her.

The man turned on him. "Get your black hands off that woman! What you trying to pull, nigger!"

Shock rocked Bunty back. His hands fell to his sides. He started to speak, but the fat man was yelling.

"You northern niggers! Trying to pull something—insult a white lady! Tar and feathers is all you understand. And don't think them army clothes is going to make any difference."

Bunty wheeled and walked fast to a side street and kept on going, until he came to a small park. He found a bench and sat down. A brown and white dog ran up, tail wagging, eyes bright. Bunty scratched him behind the ears, and the dog rushed off and returned with a stick, eager for a game. For a while Bunty played with the dog. Then someone up the street whistled, and the dog ran off.

Bunty knew that he should go and find some place to eat, but his desire for the steak was gone, and he sat in the quiet park.

A patrol car pulled up to the curb and two town policemen got out and came toward him, the older one in the lead.

"Let's see your pass, boy," he said.

Bunty pulled it out and handed it to him. The policeman read it and looked at Bunty. "What are you doing here?" he asked.

"Nothing," Bunty said.

"You can't sit here. Come on, let's get going."

"Why?" Bunty demanded. "Isn't this a public park? I'm not doing anything."

The older man looked at him. "You a northern nigger, aren't you?" He wasn't unkind, just matter-of-fact. "You are in a southern city now, boy. You can't hang around in the white folks' places. You got to keep to your own. Come on, let's go."

For a moment Bunty sat looking at him, then he glanced down at his uniform. He thought about the Pacific war, and about Europe where cities burned and Nazis, boasting that they would take over the world, sent thousands of Jews to be killed in gas ovens. He would be going to one of those places soon. He wondered if his uniform would mean more there than it did here.

He got up and went ahead of the policemen to the patrol car. He got in, and they sped along the quiet streets, back through the main part of town, past the white USO, to the Negro district. The police stopped the car to let him out, and the older man turned to him.

"Now, look, boy," he said in a flat voice. "I figure you are on your first pass, and don't know better, so I'm giving you a break this time. But don't get picked up again, or there'll be trouble. You remember that, now."

"I will remember," Bunty said, and there was no expression on his face or in his voice.

Bunty had thought that the pass would be the moment of reward after hard training. But it had been, instead, a bitter experience.

He had thought that as soon as basic training was

finished, he'd be sent over seas. He soon learned that this was not the way it was in the Army. Instead of the port of New York or San Francisco, more training lay ahead. Bunty found himself learning to build roads. Along with Cranston and Meeps, he worked with pick and shovel in the hot sun. Dust from the rock crusher sifted over them. A sergeant with a bull voice to match his bull neck chewed them out every inch of the way. Then, just as suddenly as Bunty had been given a pick and shovel, he was transferred to the Army Motor Corps.

Bunty liked that. He was good with machinery and drove a truck with the skill of a professional. The day he got his GI driver's license, he felt that he had it made.

He was given leave home, and that was great, too. He felt ten feet tall when he got off the bus and elbowed his way to the subway, his barracks bag heavy on his shoulder. Then he was walking down his home street, neighbors running out to say hello. Everything happened fast. Plump, blond Mrs. Ponosak was waving a flag. Kids were swarming after him, wanting to carry his bag. His mother was crying and hugging him, taking all of his laundry out of his bag to do up. . . . His dad gave him a long, straight look, saying quietly: "How's it going, son?" And Tim Reilly, who had been the quarter back on the team his last year, stopped by, full of envy because he had been turned down by the draft board because of a trick knee. "Man, I wish I was in there with you!"

One night he went in to Times Square, plowing up and down the noisy sidewalks, filled with people, stopping for a hot dog at a corner stand, going to the Times Square USO.

A blond girl grinned at him. "Hello, soldier. How about some coffee?"

"Easy on the cow," he said, and she fixed it the way he liked. But when the dancing started, he stayed off the floor. And he was quiet when he got home that night, quiet when he took the bus back to camp the next day.

He didn't ask for passes much after he got back.

"Had the bit?" Cranston asked.

Bunty grinned. "Which bit?" he said. "I figure the enemy's over there right now. That's who I signed up to fight. I haven't changed my mind."

"Your country, right or wrong?" Cranston said, slanting a look at him.

"That's it," Bunty said. They looked at each other for a long minute.

Bunty knew that many of the men felt the same way he did. They wanted active service. Like GIs in camps all over the country, they wanted to be putting their skills and their lives on the line.

Bunty also felt the anger growing in the Negro area— the hate of men being held down and hemmed in, of men who hit the gates with passes and were counted out so white GIs could have town leave.

"Move back! Move back!" guards would shout, rifles at port arms. And the Negroes would be forced back to watch while the white GIs filled the busses. If space were left, they could have it. But if they did get to town, most places would be off limits to them.

Bunty saw Rowland, a big, lumbering boy, tear up the pass he had been given and then denied for lack of space. "I've about had it," Rowland muttered, "just about had it," as he ground the pieces under his heel. He saw Loftus pacing up and down the barracks, his mouth tight. And he saw Meeps curl up on his bunk at night and play lonely songs on his mouth organ.

Bunty went, one Sunday, to the Negro recreation hall. It was an almost empty square room. "Uncle Tom's Cabin," the men called it, knowing that the white recreation hall was big and comfortable, that there you could order a meal if you wanted a change from army chow, or just take it easy, or write letters.

Bunty walked into the room. Half a dozen Negroes were playing cards at an old table. A group was gathered around a scratchy radio, listening to a ball game. A tall Negro with a sad face was trying to draw out a tune from the ancient piano jammed in the corner. And Bunty knew that in the white area a USO group was entertaining the troops.

He walked the length of the room to the shelf that made up the Negroes' "library." A few books were lined up there along with a pile of torn comic books at the end of the shelf. Only the day before, Bunty had been on a detail that had delivered six boxes of books marked *For Our Service Men* to the white area. Not one of those boxes had been delivered to this room.

He turned back and almost ran over Cranston, who had come up behind him.

"Present arms!" Cranston grinned. "Where you headed?"

"To get a book to read."

"Like where?"

"The white recreation hall."

Cranston's face went serious. "You won't get in."

"I'm going anyway."

"Want me to go with you?"

Bunty shook his head. "I'm going alone."

For a minute Cranston stood facing him, his eyes on Bunty's. Then a small grin tugged at the corners of his mouth. "You crazy so-and-so!" he said. "Good luck to you! Give the major my best if you happen to see him."

Bunty walked out tall and easy, down the company street, past HQ, on to the road that led to the center of the camp. He crossed the main road and entered the white section. No one was in sight. All the men were at the USO show. He walked with the same easy step to the white recreation hall, where green plants grew beside the steps and a neat black-and-white sign over the door read: *Service Men's Club.*

He went up the three steps, and walked inside the

room. Only half a dozen men were there. He saw the library section to the rear and started toward it. The sergeant on duty faced him.

"What are you doing here?" he asked.

"Getting a book to read," Bunty answered.

"You crazy, buddy? This is the white recreation hall. It's off limits to you."

"I'm a service man," Bunty said. "I want to borrow a book. Then I will go back to my area."

A look of admiration showed in the sergeant's eyes. "Listen," he said. "I don't want to make trouble for you. Go on back to your area."

Bunty stood his ground. "With the sergeant's permission," he said, "I would still like to get a book."

The sergeant smothered a grin. "You know I can't help you," he said.

"Does the sergeant refuse to let me have a book?" Bunty asked.

"You know it, soldier. Okay, take off now."

Bunty had made his point. He turned and walked back to the Negro area, his mind tight with purpose. At the first opportunity, he went to Sergeant Morrison.

"I want to make a request," he said.

Morrison listened—and frowned, shaking his head.

"I can't help you," he said. "And if you try to go on with this, I better warn you—you have yards of red tape to cut through. And then it's not going to do you any good. You know that, don't you?"

Bunty nodded. "I guess I had better start to work on that tape," he said. "I'm going to see the lieutenant."

Lieutenant Wilson listened to his request. He shook his head. "I'm not putting you off," he said. "But it won't do any good. If I could do anything about facilities, I would. In fact, I've tried. But the CO doesn't agree with me, and he commands this company. He's the superior officer here, Bunty—and that's Army."

Bunty's shoulders straightened. "I request permission to see the captain," he said.

"Okay," the lieutenant said. "But don't say I didn't warn you."

Early the next afternoon, after the company had been dismissed, Bunty faced the company clerk and stated his request. The clerk referred him to the first sergeant, who said: "Okay, private. I will take your request in."

The sergeant disappeared. Bunty stood until he came back. The sergeant pointed toward the captain's office. "Go ahead," he said.

Bunty went in. He snapped to attention in front of Captain Tarbell's desk. "Private George Bunty," he said, "has permission to speak to the captain."

Captain Tarbell fixed a stern look on him. "What's the matter, private?" he asked. "What do you want?"

"Sir, I would like to call the captain's attention to the facilities in the Negro recreation hall."

Tarbell's eyes narrowed. "What is the matter with them?"

43

"Well, sir, if the captain would consider some improvements, it would help the spirit of the men."

"Are you telling me how to run this company?" Tarbell shouted.

"No, sir," Bunty said. "But if the captain would consider even the matter of books, sir. Yesterday I was on a detail that delivered books to service men on the base. If the captain could send one box to the Negro recreation hall—"

The captain's hands slapped down on the top of his desk. "What do you think we are running—a country club?" he snapped. "You have plenty of comics!"

"Sir, some of the men would like better books to read."

Captain Tarbell's face was red with rage. "Don't tell me what you need! And don't complain to me about facilities. You understand, boy?"

"Begging the captain's pardon," Bunty said quietly. "But has the captain seen the Negro recreation hall?"

Captain Tarbell's anger boiled over. "You are a trouble maker! You need a lesson. You are going to your barracks, private. You will make up a full field pack—blankets, shelter half, everything. You will put on your web belt with full canteen, first-aid kit, and bayonet. You will carry your rifle at right shoulder arms. Then you will come out and let the sergeant inspect you. You will then march the length of the company street. When you get to the far end, you will switch to high port and run back on the double. Then you will do the whole

44

thing over again, and you will keep on doing this until I myself tell you to stop. Now move out!"

Bunty snapped to attention, saluted, marched out of the captain's office, and back to the barracks.

"What happened?" Cranston asked.

"The captain didn't like my request," Bunty said. "I drew a little punishment."

"Like what?" Meeps asked. Bunty told him. "Whooo-eee!" Meeps said softly. "In this heat? Man, I hope you make it!"

"I will," Bunty said flatly.

The sergeant was waiting for Bunty on the street, and he checked him silently. He stepped back, nodding. "Good luck," he said.

Bunty slapped the rifle to his shoulder and marched down the street. To himself he was murmuring: "Hup, two, three, four. . . ." making it a kind of game.

At the end of the street he turned about, shifting his rifle to port arms in front of his chest, and trotted back the 200 yards. He was not really puffing when he got to the end and, shifting back to right shoulder arms, he marched back.

The 100 degree heat bore down. By the time he had make his twentieth trip, sweat was running off him in streams. He could feel it puddling up in his shoes, and his shirt was sticking to his back. He felt as though his steel helmet were an oven and his head was being baked inside it. He wouldn't move his hand up to wipe the sweat out of his eyes. That was not military, and he was proving something—to himself, to the men, to the brass. The straps of his pack were rubbing his shoulders raw, but all he could do was shift his arms a little to let them rub a new place. His rifle felt slippery.

The captain walked out of his office and stood watching. Then he went back inside. From the barracks windows men of Bunty's company watched, their faces closed down. Bunty kept going. There were spots in front of his eyes from the sun—little white spots that swam up across his vision and then came back to start at the bottom of his eyes again. He tried to breathe deeply, taking in the hot air of the street to get oxygen to his heart and brain so he wouldn't pass out.

"I won't pass out," he said to himself over and over. "I will march . . . *Hup, two, three, four . . . Hup, two, three, four. . . .*" His tongue seemed to be sticking to the roof of his mouth, but his mind went on counting, telling him that he could make it.

The sun was a red ball of fire. Still he kept going. Chow call came, but the men didn't move out. They stayed in the barracks, silent, willing Bunty to make it. He heard the retreat ceremony being played on the bugle from some other area, and he came stiffly to attention, facing the flag, standing there until the last note died away. Then he moved forward again. He thought of the bugle blowing for the attack, and the Stars and Stripes waving in the wind, and all that it stood for. He kept going. He would keep on until he dropped dead, if he had to. That was the only way Tarbell could beat him . . . by killing him.

Captain Tarbell came out of his office again, and stood watching, his eyes angry. He turned suddenly and marched over to Sergeant Morrison. He spoke to him briefly. Morrison snapped to attention, and then moved fast to the company street. Bunty almost ran over him, too tired to see him.

"Okay, soldier," he said. "That's all."

"Captain said—until he—himself gave the order," Bunty said thickly, and started past him.

"It's the captain's orders, Bunty," Morrison said.

"Himself. . . ." Bunty muttered, and marched past.

And somehow he kept on until the captain stepped out, furious, and gave the order: "Dismissed, soldier!"

CHAPTER 4

Jumping-off Place

With a last stumbling effort, Bunty made it into the barracks. His knees buckled and he would have fallen, but Cranston's arm was around him. Meeps was on the other side. They got him to his bunk and stripped the damp clothes from him. Krane, a tall, quiet man with the big capable hands of a farmer, brought wet towels and they sponged Bunty's body down. He was dead asleep before they had finished.

In the days that followed, Captain Tarbell piled on discipline. It was as though he blamed the entire unit for Bunty's actions. Men muttered among themselves. Two men went AWOL—absent without leave—and then another. Krane requested leave because his wife was sick, and was denied it. He went over the hill, too.

Bunty tried to keep up the men's spirits, urging them not to break—to be tough, to stay with it. He believed that if the men stuck it out, they would be thought of not as Negroes, but as good soldiers. He wanted them to get to Germany. If they couldn't fight the feeling against them in their own country, then they would fight it in another part of the world.

"Hang in there," Bunty pleaded.

"You hang in there," Loftus shot back. "You have been brown-nosing your way through this camp since the day you got here. Well, let me tell you something. Those white officers aren't going to rub my face in the mud and get 'yes sir' and 'thank you, sir' from me!"

The words stung. Bunty turned away. He felt Loftus was wrong. He hoped the rest of the men thought so too—thought it was better to put up with things the way they were and get over seas, where the United States was fighting a war. It was their country, too. If they didn't all pitch in and fight, the United States might not win—then everybody would lose, black and white alike.

But there was a lot happening—a lot that was hard to take. One more thing, Bunty feared, might do it.

Trouble came three weeks later. Suddenly all Negro town leaves were taken away. The men were confined to their area.

"What did we do now?" Meeps demanded.

Bunty did not know, but he was determined to find out. He went straight to Morrison. Morrison told him, "There was some trouble in town."

"What kind of trouble?" Bunty asked in a flat voice.

"Johnson got in a fight with a white policeman. He tried to use a 'white only' toilet. He's in the guard house."

Bunty knew you could walk for blocks in town without finding a toilet Negroes could use. And he knew that the captain's order confining them all to the area for such a reason would set off trouble.

He went to his lieutenant, tried to explain his feelings, the men's feelings. The lieutenant understood, Bunty was sure, but he was helpless. Bunty asked to see Captain Tarbell. Permission was denied.

Back in the barracks the word was out. Bunty and Cranston and some of the others tried to hold the men back, knowing the Negroes themselves would be hurt most.

But there was no stopping them. The riot began. Bed clothes were thrown from bunks, equipment tossed on the floor. Men rushed for the gates, grabbing any weapons they could find. Loftus was in the lead, urging the men on. Bunty tried to stop him, but he turned furiously and swung his club, smashing it down on Bunty's head.

When Bunty came to, he was in the hospital. Bandages covered his head, and tape held broken ribs together. A white doctor looked down at him.

"So you finally decided to come back to the land of the living!" he said, grinning.

"How long have I been here?" Bunty asked thickly.

"Three days," the doctor said. "And you are going to be here a lot longer."

As his strength came back, Bunty had plenty of time to think. He lay staring at the green ceiling, and he thought about the war, and why he had joined up, and about the strength of men's hopes. He thought of some of the great Negro soldiers in history who had given their lives for their country. Crispus Attucks was the first American to die under British fire in the Boston Massacre. Jesse Clipper had been a hero in World War I. Negroes turned the tide at the Battle of New Orleans, and Andrew Jackson had told them: *"To the Men of Color—Soldiers! . . . I expected much from you . . . I knew that you loved the land of your birth. But you were better than I ever hoped."*

Bunty was stirred by those words. He thought of other Negro troops who had served in other wars. He thought of General Pershing, honored by all Americans, who was called 'Black Jack' because he commanded a brave Negro company. And of Benjamin Davis, the Negro ace, son of the only Negro brigadier general in the Army's history, who was writing a proud record in the Air Force. Did Captain Tarbell know about these Negro heroes? Bunty was sure he didn't.

He wondered if the rest of his army life would be one Captain Tarbell after another. What good had it done him to protest their treatment? Maybe only that it had proved he wouldn't give in. But was that enough?

Bunty began to think about the Air Force. It seemed to be one place where a Negro had a better chance.

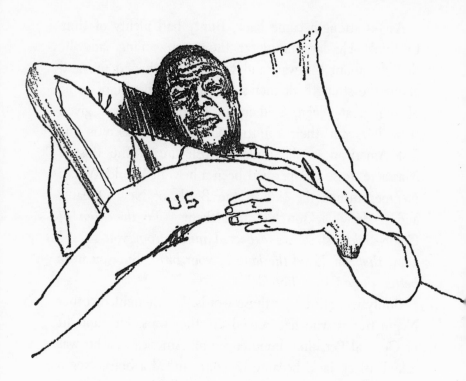

"It's the best way to get into the fight," Bunty thought. He made up his mind to apply for transfer.

There were long days of waiting after he put in his application, but Bunty hung on to hope. And then, the day before he was to be dismissed from the hospital, the word came.

"Orders for you, private." The sergeant handed them to him.

Quickly Bunty read the typed pages and found his name: Private George Bunty, 32154185, *transferred to School for Cooks and Bakers.*

His shout echoed through the ward, and a doctor came running. Bunty slammed his orders to the floor.

"Get me out of here!" he yelled. "I'm fighting those orders right down the line! That's Tarbell's doing!"

They let him out the next day, but his protest did no good. He was shipped to Texas, and his training for cook and baker began. He wouldn't quit. He kept demanding to be heard. His new CO liked his nerve. He couldn't transfer him to the Air Force as Bunty wanted, but he put through orders that sent him to Arizona for desert training. And now Bunty could hope that maybe he would be sent to Africa.

He baked at 120 degrees in the day time, and shivered at night, when temperatures dropped. Hot sand burned through the soles of his desert boots and gritted in his food. Snakes coiled in front of his pup tent, and lizards got into his bed roll. He didn't care. This was his chance to get into action.

Without warning, Bunty was suddenly transferred to Oregon, then to a service unit in Wyoming. It seemed to him that he would spend the whole war shipping back and forth across the United States. Then on February 26, 1944, the word came: *Report to Boston.*

This had to be it. Boston was the jumping-off place. As the train, full of soldiers, sped across the country, clicking off the miles, Bunty let his hopes rise. Where was he headed? England? Africa? He wondered about

Meeps and Cranston and some of the others. Where were they now? Were they on their way, too?

"Hey, men!" he thought. "Wherever you are, good luck."

On the tenth day in Boston orders were read out: "All men will receive 48-hour passes beginning at 0800 tomorrow."

Happily, Bunty packed a small bag. He would have time to get home and say good-by to his folks. He went to bed looking forward to his pass.

At three A.M. a whistle shrilled. "Come on—shake a leg! Get moving!" a sergeant shouted. "All leaves are off. Rise and shine! Move now!"

For a second it didn't sink in, and then excitement began to mount as the men realized that they were shipping out. The sergeant came in, issuing orders: "Turn in all blankets to the supply room. Take your bags to the company street and fall in!"

Lights blazed on the street. Men formed up and climbed into trucks that were wheeled into position. The trucks rumbled through the sleeping city to the port, where the men were marched through a large building on the dock. At the far end, the gang plank of a ship was lowered to the pier.

A Red Cross truck was pulled up there, and men dropped out of the ranks to get coffee and doughnuts.

"Good luck, soldier!" The girl who handed Bunty his coffee smiled.

The sergeant was checking names for the last time. Officers moved about, issuing orders, and Bunty found himself heading up the gang plank, loaded with his gear.

They moved to the rear of the main deck, and then through a metal door down into the depths of the ship and into a large room. Rows of metal frames with canvas cots laced to them took up all the space, except for narrow lanes just wide enough for the men to pass through. There was confusion as the men tried to push themselves and their gear into the small space.

"Turn in until we get under way," the sergeant ordered. Bunty got a bunk in the second row, and edged into it. Lying on his back, his nose was inches from the bunk above him, where a big man named Jim Baxter was trying to fit himself in. Below him Willy Cooper, a farm boy from Texas, was declaring that he didn't trust any ship.

Then the big engines began to pound. Everybody stopped talking. The ship began to creak and move. They were under way.

They ran silently, all lights blacked out. And as they moved out to sea, other troop ships fell into position around them. Together they headed across the ocean— their numbers protection against enemy submarines that might try to hunt them down.

On the fifth morning out, Bunty was awakened by the shrill sound of the ship's whistle and the deep pom . . . pom-pom of the big guns being fired. He jumped from his cot. Soldiers clogged the small space, rushing toward the exit. The sergeant shouted orders. Bunty wondered whether it was an enemy attack or just practice.

The deck shook under his feet. Next to him, Willy shouted, "We are going down! This is it, man!"

But the ship kept moving. Somewhere from off the port side, Bunty heard the thump of depth charges, and water spouted up. Another depth charge exploded, and another, and then an oil film spread on the surface. A submarine must have been attacking, Bunty realized. The oil indicated that the ship had scored a direct hit. The ship's all-clear sounded. Bunty gulped in a deep breath. He had had his first taste of the war.

"I sure wish I was back on dry land," Willy groaned, and all along the line, men echoed the thought.

But there were many days to go yet. On deck, soldiers from all outfits mingled and talked, shared their fear, looked forward to whatever lay ahead. There were no color lines.

But Bunty noticed that when duties were assigned, it was the Negroes who got KP, who had the last chow call for food that was often cold or in short supply, in a mess hall that smelled of men who had been sick before them. It was always the Negroes who cleaned up.

CHAPTER 5

"Black Soldiers Are Not Like Men"

Fourteen days after they had left Boston they slid into the port of Glasgow, Scotland. Scotland, the British Isles —England. The ally whose soldiers and air men had been fighting the Germans since 1939. George Bunty was in a country whose towns and harbors were being bombed by German planes flying high in the night sky.

The men moved through darkness up to the top deck. Feeling their way, they jumped on to tugs that took them to shore. There was no moon, and the black-out was like a curtain all around them.

They marched quite a distance, and then were herded into a blacked-out train. The train began to move, and then picked up speed. It was a strange feeling to speed through the unknown country, not able to see anything.

"Gives me the creeps," Willy said. "I got the feeling

those Nazi planes are right up there somewhere, ready to hit us."

The journey proved safe enough. They made several stops, but they were not allowed off the train, and they could see nothing. Then at a final stop it was their turn. The sunlight seemed very bright as they marched into it. The air smelled good.

British trucks picked them up and took them to their camp, rows of huts set in the familiar pattern of company streets, of mess hall and supply room. They learned that they were at Plymouth, where great buildings were stored with important supplies, and almost every day the German planes came over, trying to destroy them.

"You'll get used to it," a British sergeant said. Bunty wondered if he would.

They were at lunch the next day when the alarm signal screamed. The slit trenches along the sides of the street filled almost instantly with soldiers, some still holding their mess kits. It seemed forever that they lay there before they heard the engine beat of the planes and the high whine of falling bombs. The earth shook under them. Somebody prayed out loud.

But the British sergeant had been right. They soon learned to wait for the sound of the falling bombs and to guess whether the hit would be close or far. Like the British, they didn't take cover unless it was near.

Boats and trains filled with supplies arrived at Plymouth. The trains pulled straight into the buildings where the supplies were taken off. It was hard work and often for long hours, but the men felt the importance of what they were doing. Some day before long, the material stored in the large buildings would help drive back Hitler's armies.

They had been there only two weeks when Bunty's company was suddenly moved up to London. He was assigned to truck duty, transporting supplies from the docks to the storage depots. He got his first glimpse of the city, and war was suddenly very real.

In some blocks buildings looked as though they had not been touched, but in others great holes showed where bombs had hit. Piles of brick stood where buildings had once been. Store windows were boarded up. Brilliant beams of light stabbed through the darkness when plane alarms came, searching for enemy craft. Ack-ack fire exploded, and RAF planes moved in to drive off the enemy.

Bunty had had no leave since his arrival, and he was excited when he got his first 48-hour pass. All he had known of the city so far was his truck route, and now he set out to see the sights. There was Big Ben that he had read about, and Hyde Park, and Buckingham Palace.

Even the war couldn't wipe out the city's beauty. Or the people's kindness. Bunty was touched when he found that Londoners welcomed the Negro soldiers as well as the whites. A small boy ran up and insisted on shining his shoes—free. An old lady selling flowers on a corner tucked a flower in his button-hole.

"That's for you, Yank," she said. "Get along with you and have a good time!"

He walked happily along the streets, feeling good. He came to a bar, and through the window he could see some men playing darts. It would be fun to go in, he thought, but he hesitated. In spite of the friendly people, he wasn't sure whether such places allowed Negroes, and he did not want to risk being turned away.

As he stood there trying to make up his mind, a plump, smiling middle-aged man came up to him. "I say, lad, your first leave in London?"

Bunty nodded. The man put out his hand and shook Bunty's warmly. "Chester's the name," he said. "Glad to have you here with us. Come along inside, and I will stand you to a half-n-half—you know, ale and beer."

Bunty went with him gladly. The little man talked about Churchill and FDR and how the British had hoped the Yanks would come into the war. He asked all kinds of questions about America, and Bunty told him stories about home. They played darts for a while with some of the other Englishmen. It was a good afternoon.

In April, Bunty's company was moved suddenly to a camp near a small town in the north of England. It was a gasoline depot—thousands of cans of gas, badly needed, were stacked as high as a building in a huge field. Trains filled with the cans came in after dark. The trains had to be emptied by morning and the nets to hide the cars put back in place before daylight. The German Air Force would have liked nothing better than to find this depot and destroy it.

The men drove themselves hard, faces gleaming with sweat in the cold night air. Cans moved fast down the line. Men caught them as they were tossed up, and put them in place. *"Come on . . . hup . . . on the double! That sun's going to be showing in two hours!"*

Gray light began to break in the sky. Men scrambled to get the nets up. The train pulled out fast, and men raced to hide the tracks.

There were nights when the train didn't come in, and the men had time on their hands. But passes to town were hard to get, and the few men who got them usually came back before their time was up.

"Nothing to do there. Man, that town's shut tight to GIs."

Bunty couldn't understand it. The British people in Plymouth and London had been so friendly. Why had things changed here?

He got a pass and went to town himself. It was a pretty village with narrow, crooked streets and small shops. The people looked nice, but they seemed to avoid him—even to fear him. A mother hurried her children indoors when he went down their street. All the shops and the bars had signs posted on the doors: *Off Limits to Service Men.*

Upset, Bunty walked to the edge of town and sat on

61

a stone wall, looking out across the fields, which were just beginning to get green. He was suddenly longing for home.

A young girl on a bicycle rounded the curve in the road. She saw him sitting there, and with a small cry tried to turn back too quickly. The bicycle went out of control, and she fell heavily.

Bunty ran to her. She tried to scramble away, but her knee was cut and her skirt caught in the bicycle's gears.

"Here, let me help you," Bunty said. He stopped the flow of blood with his handkerchief. Carefully he freed her skirt and lifted the bicycle away.

"Don't hurt me," she whispered.

Bunty stared at her. "Why should I hurt you?"

When she didn't answer, he took the handkerchief from her and, going to the ditch by the road, wet it and brought it back. Carefully he washed away the blood.

"It's not too bad a cut," he said. "But you should put something on it when you get home." He sat back on his heels, looking at her steadily. "Why did you think I would hurt you?" he asked again.

"They told us to be careful," she said in a low voice.

He frowned. "Who told you?"

"The officers. The white officers. They came before the camp was set up. And they said—"

She stopped. Bunty could feel the knot in his stomach, but he kept his voice quiet. "What did they say?"

64

"That the black soldiers are—not like men. That they rob and hurt people."

Bunty stood up slowly. "That's not true," he said.

She looked at him. "Have I tried to hurt you?" he asked her. "Has any man from the camp hurt anyone?"

She shook her head. He held out his hand. After a moment, she took it, and he helped her to her feet. Touching his fingers to his cap, he started off.

"Wait!" she called suddenly.

He hesitated and then turned, and she came up to him. She stood for a moment looking up at his face, and then she said: "I'm sorry."

"Thank you," he said. And then, nodding good-by again, he set off back to camp.

The anger was cold in him now. He said nothing of what he had learned to the other men, but that afternoon he wrote to General Headquarters, telling the story.

Two weeks later a group of official visitors arrived in the camp. They came by car, and they walked with military step into the camp's headquarters. In the lead was Brigadier General Benjamin Davis, the highest ranking Negro in the United States Army. What he said to the CO was never known, but the official party made a trip to the village that afternoon, the CO with them. The off-limits signs came down, the fears were quieted.

On his return to camp, General Davis reviewed the troops. They snapped to attention, each man in the ranks proud of the general's record. And he stood in front of them and praised their work and their loyalty.

That night the men sang as they worked. Gas cans slapped from hand to hand. Men cheered as each row was set up. They finished in record time.

"Come on, you Jerries!" Baxter yelled. "You won't find this dump. It's going to be driving our tanks right into Berlin!"

The fear was gone from the town now, but Bunty's company had little time to enjoy the village. The gas depot they had worked on was filled. They moved on.

Bunty was driving a truck again, moving supplies toward the port areas. Everywhere there was the feeling of build-up. Nobody knew where the attack would be opened, but they knew it would not be too long now.

And then they were moving into a staging area. Moving at night, without being warned—just as they had moved at ship-out time from Boston—in trucks that rumbled up the road. Curtains were down, and it was hot in the trucks. Willy Cooper stirred beside Bunty. "You think they'll fly us in?"

Bunty shook his head. "How could they fly enough men in?" he asked. "They'll take us in boats."

The Texas boy moaned. "I'm not going on any boat. Not after that last one."

Bunty grinned. "You better break out your water wings, then," he said. "Looks like you'll be swimming."

The staging area was set in a stand of trees. Security was tight. Guards were at every entrance, and nobody could go in or out of the camp. Orders came to wear uniforms that were treated against poison gas. They felt stiff and smelled funny, and Bunty thought suddenly of the day they had gone into the 'gas chamber' at Rushmore.

Now every day seemed a year long. At night the blackout was complete—thick, close, heavy darkness, without a spot of light anywhere. Above them they could hear the German planes, and then the RAF planes, and in the distance, the dull sound of bombing.

"I wish we would get out of here," Bunty thought.

Still they waited . . . the last days of May, the first days of June. The weather turned bad. It was cold and stormy. Nerves grew tighter.

Then on June 6, 1944, like an electric current, the news passed through the camp: *D-Day! The Allies have landed in France.*

A distant roar echoed across the Channel. The sky beat with the sound of RAF planes, swarming toward the coast of France in air cover. And out there on the black, cold waters of the English Channel, thousands of boats crossed in the darkness, and men struggled ashore.

The camp heard no more news.

"They have to get through," Bunty told himself.

In every man's mind that night was a picture of flat-bottomed boats filled with men, of waves of soldiers struggling to hit the coast and make it up the cliffs, of enemy gun fire stabbing at them.

"We are going to find out real soon what it's like," Jim Baxter said. "I got the feeling."

"All I want is to get going," Bunty said. "Those guys over there need us. Who's going to get the supplies in if we sit here on our tails?"

Twenty-four hours later, just at dusk, the blast of the sergeant's whistle called them to action. Nobody had to tell them what this was.

Full field packs were strapped on, helmets buckled. Troops formed up. Shouts echoed: *"Fall in! Fall in!"*

And then they moved out of the staging area, down the hill toward the sea where hundreds of boats were at anchor, waiting.

They marched through the streets of the town. Women and children stood in doorways, their faces serious, watching them go. The clump of boots sounded on the stone streets. A group of Spitfire planes roared overhead.

Bunty realized that his hand was damp against his rifle. Up ahead, the sergeant hupped them along and, softly at first, then more strongly, the men picked it up.

And so they marched, down to the loading area. Spray from the rough sea spit at them. Rain had begun to fall.

Bunty found himself on the slippery deck of a boat, kneeling between crates of shells and rolls of wire. As far distant as he could see in the fading light, men and supplies were being loaded onto boats. Half-track trucks ground their way into cargo holds.

And then they set out on the rough sea. Boats rocked and churned. Men were sick where they stood or sat, packed tightly into place, unable to move. The rain turned to a sudden storm that beat down.

Bunty willed himself to go to sleep. He was going to need every ounce of strength he had tomorrow. The boat seemed to churn under him, and he wanted to be sick, but he wouldn't let himself. At last he fell asleep.

He woke with a start at early dawn. He realized suddenly that the engines weren't running, and all he could hear was the slap of the waves against the boat. Stiffly he crawled out of his cramped place. All he could see were gray clouds and gray sea. The sky began to grow light. Other men came awake. An officer shouted at them to break out their food rations, and those who weren't too sick did. Bunty wasn't hungry, but he made himself eat his processed ham and eggs. It was like eating cardboard.

The boat's engine roared suddenly, and now they were leaving a churning wake at the stern. Everything seemed to come alive. They were rushing directly at the beach.

Bunty could see Omaha Beach now. It was littered with burned-out tanks. Bodies lay on the sand where they had fallen. Other tanks were stuck in the wet sand. Knocked-out landing boats rocked in the water. Bunty moved forward and looked at the ugly sea, a film of oil on its surface. Just below he saw the body of a GI floating face down and, as he looked, it disappeared suddenly under the boat.

Boats were moving into landing positions, the Higgins boats first, hatched out of the big, clumsy transports. Craft were having trouble finding openings. Boats that had been sunk clogged the way. Troops had been able to blast only a few openings. Bunty's boat found one, and they pushed through.

Naval guns thundered near them. From the cliffs above the beach, a German gun kept up a rattle of fire.

"Form up! Form up!" the lieutenant was ordering, and Bunty shifted into position for the beach run. A little to the left of them a boat went in ahead, and Bunty saw the men hit the water, struggling with heavy loads. A fast-moving wave struck at them, and two men went under and were held with their heads down by the weight of their loads and their life belts' floating power. He saw them drown, and in one swift move he snaked off his life belt and thrust it over his right arm.

"Carry it this way!" he yelled. "It won't pull you under, but it will still float you!"

On deck other men moved quickly to follow his lead. Bombers roared over their heads and black clouds mushroomed up. Their boat pushed forward and hit bottom, throwing men off their feet. They scrambled back to position at the commands of the officers.

Then they were moving off the boat, rolls of wire

and crates of shells on their shoulders. A German Stuka plane came in, firing, and the cold water around them shot up in angry bursts. The man behind Bunty screamed suddenly and disappeared under the water.

"Hand pass! Hand pass!" Bunty shouted, and the men struggling toward shore began to pass the supplies from one to another. "Move!" Bunty grunted, shoving a roll of wire at the man ahead of him. "Come on, move!"

He was scared. Never had he known he could be this scared. But he was moving and so were the others.

His feet hit a rise of sand, and he staggered up it, half realizing that he was on the beach. He wanted to fall flat and get his breath back. But there was no time. He found himself grabbing crates of shells, wire, anything he could get his hands on, and rushing up the beach. Bulldozers already carved out paths through the brush on top of the bluffs. German planes came in, and he threw himself against the cliff for protection.

Nobody counted the hours, morning, noon, or night. Troops streamed ahead, following openings made by the D-Day forces. But they couldn't keep going if supplies didn't get in. Bunty and the other men in his unit bent their backs to the job.

Sometime toward the end of the next day, Bunty crawled into a fox hole and fell dead asleep.

CHAPTER 6

Omaha Beach

Bunty woke up cramped and stiff, with the sun beating down on his face, his rifle lying across him. He heard the boom of heavy guns in the distance, and felt the earth tremble as a bomb exploded.

Slowly he lifted his head out of the fox hole and looked around. On the bluffs and the wooded draws, bulldozers jockeyed back and forth clearing the ground. A row of trucks rumbled past. An officer's jeep wheeled by and an enemy bullet glanced off the side. In the field to his left, Bunty saw a German sign: *Achtung Minen!* Danger—Mines. The Germans had planted exploding mines in the ground. Any soldier who stepped on one would be blown up.

Bunty had no idea where his outfit was. The last he knew was when he had dropped in his tracks, bone tired. He eased himself out of the fox hole and headed toward what seemed to be the center of activity. A sergeant stopped him, and he gave his name, rank, and number. The sergeant shoved a thumb in the direction he should go, and he found his unit in an old German fort.

It was a shock to find how his company had been cut up. Baxter was dead, Willy had been wounded and moved to a hospital in England. Many others were missing.

Sergeant Watts, who was in charge, grinned when he saw Bunty. "See you made it," he said. "Eat some chow and report back."

Bunty realized suddenly how hungry he was. He sat down, wolfing his C-rations, and boiled some coffee in his canteen cup. No one seemed to know for sure how the fighting was going. Other men from Bunty's company began to come in. Each arrival raised the men's spirits.

"Okay, okay!" the sergeant barked. "You going to sit around all day, talking? There's a war on!"

They were assigned to take supplies off the ships that had just arrived. Craft were having trouble getting through the clogged beach approaches. Work boats with big cranes dipped and lifted. Men set charges under the dead craft, blasting them into the air. On the bluffs, engineers were leveling an air strip, and trucks and columns of men headed for the front over roads that crews were still repairing. On the hill across the draw, the dead lay in white mattress covers, waiting to be buried.

Bunty lost all sense of time. It didn't matter. When chow came, it was time to eat. When no craft could get through, it was time to sleep in the fox hole he had dug beside the others. The fox holes stretched for nearly a mile, and every night when the German Air Force—Luftwaffe—came over, the holes were the soldiers' protection. Bunty found some pieces of wood and roofed his fox hole over.

"All the comforts of home," a bony, light-skinned Negro named Jim Parker said.

Bunty grinned. "With hot and cold running water."

By the end of the week, Omaha Beach was cleared up. Bulldozers had pushed the burned-out trucks, the tangles of wire, into a huge ditch. Off the shore, a line of Liberty ships had been sunk to make a heavy break water, and rhino ferries, hatched from the hulls of LCTs, churned into the beach. Columns of soldiers marched toward the beach exits. Everything was moving fast.

"You start driving a two-and-a-half tomorrow," the lieutenant told Bunty one night.

"Yes, *sir!*" Bunty said.

Parker was assigned as his helper. They headed out at 0600 in a long line of trucks. Choking white dust sifted down through the hatch in the top of the cab above Parker's head, cut there so he could get at the machine gun mounted above them.

They pushed their way through the town of Isigny, now in ruins. The smell of dead fish was strong.

"Worse than the Jersey dumps!" Bunty said.

74

Parker laughed. "How would you like to be smelling them right now?"

From off shore, an Allied battle ship shelled the flats where the Nazis had dug in. The boom seemed to shake the truck. The rattle of small-arms fire came from somewhere off to their left, where GI's were cleaning out a pocket of Germans.

Parker was itching to use the machine gun, and he kept sticking his head out the hatch to see if he could spot an enemy plane flying low near the road.

"They saw you coming!" Bunty said. "They've all gone back to Hitler."

They barreled through a small village, and the French people on the street cheered as they thundered past. A few miles farther along, the driver ahead of him flagged for a stop, and Bunty jammed on the brakes. Without the rattle of the trucks, the sound of shelling was louder.

"They must mean business up there," Parker said, and Bunty nodded.

An MP came over to their truck. "You are coming into the front line area," he said. "The route to your supply dump is flagged. Follow your leader. Okay, move."

Bunty jammed the truck into gear. The truck ahead of him was already moving, and he gunned his after it. As they streamed out onto the open flat, Bunty's hands closed hard on the wheel. He felt like a sitting duck.

Ahead of them, a stand of trees loomed. The sense of protection under the trees felt good. A hundred yards

in, they came to a stop. They had reached the supply dump. At the far edge of the woods, a regiment was shelling the enemy ahead, softening them up for an attack. They could her the smack of bullets against trees and the whine of shells as the Germans fired back.

Orders were passed along the truck line. Sweating and grunting, the men bent their backs to remove the supplies from the trucks. The wounded were already being brought up. As fast as a truck was emptied, they were placed aboard. The headed back for Omaha Beach.

The third day out, they were fired on by a plane. Trucks ahead jammed to a halt, pulling off the road to cover if they could. Men in the trucks that weren't armored dove for the ditches. With a yell, Parker was through the cab hatch, swinging the gun into position.

The ME-109 came in, engine screaming, fire spitting from its guns. A stream of bullets chattered along the row of trucks. The plane banked, wheeled, and came in again. Parker's gun fired back. The gun four trucks ahead had been knocked out, and a soldier's body lay on the cab roof. From the ditches someone was screaming.

"Ammo!" Parker yelled. Bunty fed a belt of shells into the gun. "Come on, you—" The plane dove again.

The plane came straight down the road, the guns along its wings winking like small danger lights. Bullets arched down into the string of trucks, kicking dirt up on both sides of the column, and tearing through truck cabs and engines. Black smoke and then flame shot up from some place down the line as a gas tank was hit.

Parker began firing when the plane was less than 1000 yards away, aiming just in front. The pilot pulled sharply up and out, but it was too late. Bunty could see holes in the plane, and a film of oil spraying backward away from the plane. Parker flung himself around in the hatch, keeping his gun bearing on the ME. Flame and black smoke shot from the ship. With a roar the enemy craft burst in half, wings and engine turning end over end in the air, then exploding into a field. Fragments of the wrecked plane flew upward in all directions.

"I got him! I got him!" Parker yelled, sweat running down his face. Along the road, men were coming out from ditches and under trucks.

Bunty took his first-aid kit from his belt, and ran to the nearest wounded man. He did what he could and moved on to the next man. All along the road, those who had gotten out free were helping those who had been hurt. Some were beyond help. The wounded were left to the medics—first-aid men—the knocked-out trucks for repair units. The other trucks went on.

D-Day plus 19—19 days after D-Day—the gale began. The sky was the color of lead. In the Channel, waves hit against the scarred bluffs at Omaha Beach. Trucks fought their way from beach supply dumps through deep mud. By the end of the first day, traffic was stalled.

For two more days the storm raged. Craft piled up in tangled heaps on the shore. The artificial harbor that had been set up buckled and began to give way. With others, Bunty stood staring at the mess, thinking about the GIs in the front lines. Without enough supplies, what could they do?

An air lift was started, but it could only bring in 500 tons of bullets and supplies a day. Bunty and Parker

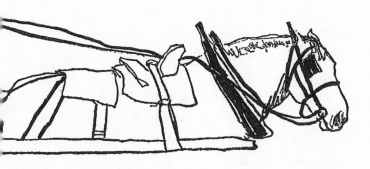

were pulled off duty, and 12 hours later, new orders came for their entire outfit. They were being shifted to a labor group south of them to set up a rest area.

"How come us?" Parker asked.

"Some guy in HQ was looking for strong backs and our number came up," Bunty said.

Parker shot a look at him. "Don't you mean strong *black* backs?"

Bunty couldn't argue. "So it's a job that has to be done," he said. He kicked a tin can with fury.

It was a bitter pill. At the new location, Bunty helped clear the area, hauling in supplies. He spoke to no one.

Bunty and Parker went to town one night, catching the company truck. The driver stopped near the main street. "Okay," he said. "Be here at 2300 for a lift to camp."

They walked down the street and turned into a *café*. Old men sat drinking wine, women chatted. Some pretty girls smiled and tried to talk to them in French.

The owner of the *café* brought Bunty and Parker French bread and bowls of good onion soup. Everyone was friendly. People began to sing, and the boys joined in. All at once Bunty looked at his watch. "Holy smoke!" he said to Parker. "We've missed the truck."

"What is wrong?" an old man asked, and Bunty told him. "Wait here," he said.

He hurried away. Soon he was back with a donkey cart. Bunty and Parker climbed in and, to the cheers of the village people, they set off.

They made it back in good time, and Bunty and Parker scrambled down from the cart. "*Merci!*" they shouted. "Thanks! Thanks!"

With a wave, the old man took off, and they hurried into the camp, feeling better than they had since they had been sent there.

CHAPTER 7

Signed Up to Fight

The last delivery was brought in. Cherbourg, just southwest of Omaha Beach, was open now and new supplies would be coming there. Bunty was transferred there and put into a dock outfit, taking the tons of supplies for the front line off the boats.

The weather turned wet and cold. Chilling rain dripped off coats and caps. The wind was raw, and it seemed to Bunty he would never be warm and dry again.

Off duty, he poured a cup of water he had heated into his helmet and put a piece of soap in it. He soaked his socks and squeezed them out.

"All you have to do is dry them now," Parker said.

Bunty looked toward where the kitchen was set up. Wet socks in hand, he walked over and asked, "How about letting me put up a line behind the stove and dry these?"

"You nuts?" the cook yelled. "You want your mashed potatoes to taste like old socks? Go on, get lost!"

Bunty eased his way in and, before long, had his line up and his socks drying. Twenty minutes later, there was a rush to the cook house and every man had a pair of wet socks in hand.

"Get out of here!" the cook yelled, throwing a pot at the lead man. "Bunty! B-u-u-nty! Get those socks out of here before I cook them and serve them to you on a shingle!"

But Bunty had suddenly gone deaf. That night he and the others put on the first dry socks they had had in days.

In October new orders came, and Bunty's outfit moved toward the front. Their route was around Paris, and all the men hung out of the trucks, wishing they could have a pass to go there. Past Reims, where they glimpsed the great cathedral still standing, through Belgium and into Holland. Near Zundert they were assigned to work at a supply dump, emptying trucks, guarding the supplies, signing them out to the fighting men.

Ahead of them they could hear the roar and rumble of the 88's, the crack of machine gun fire. Buildings were burning in the city. The earth shook as bombs exploded.

"The Krauts are getting it," a supply sergeant grinned, mopping his face. "Break out a couple of cases of 81-mm shells for me. Okay?"

Bunty put the shells onto the truck. "Give them a blast for me," he said.

"Will do," the sergeant answered. He scratched his name on the receipt Bunty gave him, and took off.

Troops were moving ahead fast. Supply lines had to be made shorter. Bunty's company moved forward, near the Maas River.

"Let's get set up!" the sergeant yelled. "Let's—"

The sharp crack of a rifle cut off his words. The sergeant spun, arms stretched wide, and fell heavily. Bunty's rifle was in his hand, his eyes searching. Bullets spit from a tree, tearing off a handful of leaves, and Bunty fired. He felt the shock of a bullet smashing into his leg, and he grunted in pain. He squeezed off a shot. A high scream sounded above the crack of rifles, and the body of a German fell to earth.

Pain stabbed through Bunty as he ran to the sergeant. Blood soaked his pants leg. The sergeant was dead.

Parker hurried toward him. "You've been hit." He had his first-aid kit out, fumbling it open.

"Get the stuff off the trucks," Bunty yelled. "I'm okay!"

He wadded his handkerchief up and stuffed it against the wound, grabbed the bandage roll from Parker's kit, and tied it in place. A lieutenant had men beating the bushes for other Germans, and three were herded out, hands above their heads. They were pushed onto one of the trucks and moved out.

The last case was off the trucks, the last net in place before Bunty would stop. Then he sat down suddenly on the ground. His whole leg felt on fire, and he was dizzy from loss of blood. But when a first-aid man reached him, he tried to wave him away.

"Go on, take care of somebody that needs it," he grunted. "I just got nicked a little."

"You just got yourself a pass out of here," the first-aid man told him, putting medicine on the wound. "You've had it for a while, Bud."

At the field hospital, Bunty's wound was dressed. In vain he argued that he would be okay in a couple of days. "Don't send me out of here," he pleaded.

He was still arguing when they put him on a truck, heading to a base hospital, and then to a rest area.

"Of all the bad luck," he muttered, as he crawled into his bunk the first night.

The guy next to him grinned. "You haven't seen anything yet," he said. "Welcome to the black man's Miami. And see you keep off the *White Only* side."

Bunty found that it was true. The rest area was segregated. On the white side, a large recreation hall stood. For the Negroes, there was a small "Uncle Tom's Cabin." Days were long. Time hung heavy on the men's hands.

"I got a notion to go AWOL," Hodges, an Alabama boy, muttered. "What am I getting out of this war?"

"You go AWOL over here, you are in real trouble," Bunty said.

"So what?" Hodges answered, but he didn't take off.

Bunty had never felt so low. He started a letter home, and then tore it up. What was there to write about?

When his wound healed, he was returned to his unit. The weather had been bad and got worse. Snow fell, and the temperature dropped. Still, Bunty was glad he was back on duty. At least there was a purpose to the work he did.

They were in the rolling hills of Aachen now, and the Germans held on to every foot of ground. Planes pounded at enemy positions, but the Germans did not give. On December 16, 1944, the enemy began to fight back. The Battle of the Bulge had begun.

Day after day the fighting went on. And day after day the news was bad . . . *the Allies have had to retreat . . . there has been a German break through . . . a Panzer Division is massing. . . .*

Skies were gray. Fresh snow fell. Air fields were socked in, and the Allied air support couldn't get off the ground.

Bunty and the men in his unit gave all they had to handling supplies. The wounded went back by truck as the toll mounted.

Then suddenly, on December 23, the sun came out. The air began to fill with the sound of engines. Planes filled the skies—1000, 2000 planes flew their missions, searching for hidden Nazi divisions, bombing them out.

And then it was Christmas. Bundled up in his heavy jacket, Bunty ate his C-rations and grinned at Parker. "Merry Christmas," he said. "I hope those Krauts are enjoying our presents."

The German advance had been stopped, but Allied losses had been enormous. And now, during those last days of December, came news they couldn't believe: Negroes in service units would be allowed to sign up to fight!

The word spread like wild fire. Bunty let out a yell when he heard it and raced to his CO. "Private George Bunty," he said. "Signing up for active duty!"

Over 5000 Negroes signed up. The rush was so great that the order had to be taken back, or many service units would have been left with only a few men.

Then the waiting started. Each day dragged by. At last, just after New Year's, the word came: Bunty and Parker had made it. They would go to Noyon, a town fifty miles north of Paris, for training.

The camp at Noyon was a sea of activity. Men were shipping in from France, from England, from Belgium and Holland. Tents were set up. Units formed.

Bunty squeezed into the tent he had been assigned to. It was full of men. Suddenly a shout split the air, and a wiry little guy with big ears came hurtling toward him. "You old dog face!" he shouted. "I knew I was going to find you here! Whooo-eee!"

"Meeps!" Bunty thumped him on the back. "Where did you come from?"

"Same place as you," Meeps grinned. "Out there lifting those crates and loading those bales, man! Some place they call Antwerp."

Parker elbowed his way up, and Bunty introduced him. They traded stories.

"Old Schickelgruber better look out now!" Meeps laughed. "We're going to give it to him, right in der Fuehrer's face!"

They trained at Noyon under sergeants and officers who had been in battle, and the training was rough, the weather freezing cold. Nobody cared how tough the going was. They did everything asked of them and came back, asking for more.

They charged across practice fields as though to attack. They pushed through snow to the bayonet field where bags filled with straw waited. *"Thrust . . . withdraw!"*

the sergeant bellowed, and bayonets drove into the bags, over and over until men's arms ached.

"Let's take it again! That's a Kraut in front of you! *Thrust . . . thrust!*" And Bunty's bayonet drove deep.

Drill, practice, chow down, sleep, drill, practice. . . . The days ticked by.

"This is a rifle grenade," the sergeant said, holding it

up. "Slide it down over the spring-loaded tube. Got that? It's set to explode when it hits. Okay, let's try it."

Bunty loaded the blank shell used to fire the grenade and aimed. He pulled the trigger, and was knocked over backward. Men hit the dirt to escape flying fragments.

"That's lesson one," the sergeant said. "Brace yourself against the weapon. Fire at a higher angle."

It didn't take Bunty long to become expert with the grenades, but the bazooka—the Army's anti-tank gun— was tougher. It took two men to fire it, and he and Parker were teamed up, Bunty holding the tube on his shoulder and aiming it, Parker socking the rocket into the rear of the tube and attaching the wires.

Bunty squeezed the trigger. For a second, nothing happened. Then, with a red flame jetting from the rear, it went off, and Parker hit the dirt close to Bunty to keep from being burned. The bazooka had more lift than a rifle, and it took Bunty a long time to get used to it. It was a great day when he first managed to put most of his rounds where he aimed them.

"Man, we ever going to get out of here?" Meeps complained. "I want to get me a shot at a Jerry!"

Bunty grinned. "There'll be a few left for us."

Training went on. The officers, tough as they were, didn't try to hide their pride in the men they were training.

"You men know how to fight!" the lieutenant told them. "You are good because you want to be. It's too bad we didn't have you from D-Day on. Okay, dog faces, hit Y area on the double."

Y area was the small, icy river near them. The weather was at its worst. Snow caked the ground and froze to their clothes. Bunty's feet felt frozen in his boots.

At the river, a strip of ice had been blasted out, leaving a wide section of cold water. An assault crew was waiting. Metal assault boats were set in the snow on the river bank.

"Eight men to a boat, four on each side," the training officer told them. "Carry the boats to the river and put them in the water. Get aboard and cross the river. You are equipped with safety belts. Squeeze the CO_2 tube near your belt buckle if you get into trouble in the water. The belt will fill. Watch this demonstration."

The training unit raced to the boats, hauled them to the river's edge, and shot them into the water. Men were aboard, and the boats crossed swiftly down the stream to the opposite shore. It looked very simple.

"Form up!" the sergeant shouted. "You'll be under live fire this time."

The Go order snapped along the line. Bunty was between Meeps and Parker, and with their crew they rushed forward. Machine guns opened up. Bullets streamed just above their heads and hit the ground at the river bank in sprays of dirt and water. Bunty felt sweat pop out on his face in spite of the cold and, grunting and shoving, he helped move the boat forward, trying to keep down. In the crew next to them a guy hit the ground in fear. His CO_2 tube broke. Gas poured out, filling the belt, and Bunty heard his yells as he tried to get closer to the ground and away from the bullets.

Bunty's crew got their boat in the water and climbed aboard. Trouble really started then. The boat wouldn't behave. Instead of heading for the opposite shore, it went around and around.

"Paddle together!" Bunty yelled, and after what seemed forever they managed to make it. They finally hit the other bank of the river. Sergeants were waiting there to send them back, and the firing went on just over their heads.

"Now you guys see what it's like to cross a river," the lieutenant told them when it was over. "Don't think the enemy doesn't know how tough it is. They'll be stacked up somewhere trying to pick you off. But your job is to get across. Okay, let's try it again."

So they trained and grew tough, and learned. But all the men wondered when the training would end and the fighting begin.

They didn't get the word until late in March, and when it came, it wasn't quite the word they had been counting on.

"Officers from fighting units will pick up men from this company beginning at 0800 tomorrow morning. You will proceed to front-line areas where you will be attached to white units."

Bunty felt the shock of the words hit him like a blow, and along the line he heard the sucked in breaths that rippled through the ranks. They had been told when they signed up that they would be put in with fighting units—man to man. Now, in a few sentences, they learned that the promise had been broken. They would go into battle, but they would be segregated.

"Whooo-eee!" Meeps breathed softly, but no one in line moved or changed expression.

The CO stood silent in front of them for a minute.

Then he said: "Men, I'm proud of you. You've come through training with flying colors. You are soldiers in the United States Army, and good ones. Now get out there and fight! That's what this war asks of you."

Men were disappointed about the segregation order, but they were still determined to be good soldiers. That night after chow they sat around the smoking coal stoves that kept them half warm.

"Man," Meeps said quietly, "They still think black and white. But old Hitler doesn't know the difference. One of us knocks off some of his supermen, they are going to be just as dead. And he's going to say the Yanks did it. Maybe some day at home they'll give up black and white, too, and just think 'people.'"

The second day after training finished, the camp went to chow through whirling snow that was almost a blizzard. The news began to spread almost as soon as they started to eat: "Two guys went AWOL. They pulled out last night!"

Bunty felt sick. Men wouldn't look at each other. Talk was short. This couldn't have happened! Their record had been perfect. And now—two men had slipped out of camp.

"Why?" Bunty groaned. "Why did they do it?"

"Maybe it hit them too hard," Parker said quietly. "Being promised equal fighting places, and then being faced with segregation again."

"Don't you think it hit us all?" Bunty snapped. "But we didn't cave in. That's not the way to show we've got it!"

"I know," Parker said.

Bunty pounded his fist against the table. "I don't believe they ran off," he said. "I knew those guys. They were straight—they were soldiers."

"But they're gone," Parker said.

Gloom fell over the camp. Officers felt as bad as the men. The day passed slowly. At evening mess nobody was hungry. The cook came up with the old call: "Take all you want, but eat all you take!" But his heart wasn't in it.

And then the news came: *The men didn't take off!*

You know what they did? Hitch-hiked to the front and reported for duty! They couldn't wait to get fighting!

The men began to laugh. "Get those guys! They hit the front line before us, all by themselves!"

The CO marched in, a big grin on his face. "As you seem to know," he said, "Privates Wendell and Washington have reported to the front lines north of Aachen for active duty. Their actions may have been unusual, but their fighting spirit is to be admired!"

A cheer echoed off the mess hall ceiling. Hats flew into the air. The cook broke out a special treat. It was only canned peaches, but who cared?

The next day, Bunty's unit and a second one were called out early. The sergeant was there, the lieutenant, the CO. Bunty knew this was it.

The CO stepped forward. "You men go into duty today with the 104th Infantry. Men, you're joining the fighting Timber Wolves. Good luck to you!"

They had half an hour to get ready to move out, and then they were snaking their way toward the freight train that would take them to the front lines. Shell belts rode their hips. Canteens and first-aid kits were attached to their belts' eyes. Field packs were snug on their backs, and mess kits fitted into them. Rifles were in their hands, gas masks were hung over their shoulders.

"Hup! Hup!" the order came. And the men marched out to the freight cars. They were headed for the front and Bunty felt ready for battle.

CHAPTER 8

The Long Night

The train carrying Bunty and his unit rolled through the cold night of France, north, toward Cologne in Germany. The rumble of bombs reached them, and star shells and tracer bullets arched against the sky.

They were coming into the battle area. Hands gripped rifles, or reached back to settle field packs.

They were shifted to trucks, and bounced over the road. Shell fire grew louder. Bunty craned forward and then, rising black and needle sharp against the sky, he saw the Cologne Cathedral. It was a beautiful sight—the great cathedral still standing as though God Himself had protected it.

The trucks slowed down. Block on block of ruined buildings rose on each side of them, their walls still standing but floors gone, so Bunty could see through the buildings' skeletons. Piles of bricks lay in the streets.

Finally the trucks stopped and the men were ordered out.

"Okay, you guys. This is where you hitch up with the 104th. You'll be camping in the cellars along Adolf Hitler Street tonight."

Bunty climbed down out of the truck. What families had once lived here? The buildings were rat holes now.

"Come on! Move in! Move in!" a sergeant was ordering, and Bunty found himself inching his way down in.

They sat there in the dark, and some time later hot chow was brought to them. A lieutenant came in before they had finished eating.

"You men are assigned as a rifle unit to the 415th regiment. You'll move out at 0500."

Nobody slept much that night. Every sound brought the men awake. Before the appointed hour, they were ready to load up, and they climbed into the trucks.

The route lay south toward Remagen. They rumbled through small towns where people dragged children's wagons or pushed baby carts full of what was left of their goods, moving back to whatever was left them of their homes. Bunty felt a dry spot in his throat.

The trucks were close to the front now. They rumbled across a bridge built in a hurry by army engineers.

They were on the east banks of the Rhine, moving toward the hills beyond. The trucks stopped suddenly.

"All out! All out!"

Bunty jumped down over the tail gate. He could see the black hills rising all around them and the truck tops standing out against the sky. Sergeants called quietly, "To your left . . . let's move now."

They moved into the gloom, following the leader and two scouts. They began to climb, working their way up a ridge, then down a long valley. Trees on both sides shut out the sights and sounds of other units.

Ahead of them everything was quiet. It was as though they were alone on earth, but Bunty had a strange feeling of being watched. To the west, guns suddenly roared, and bright flashes showed above the hills.

Bunty heard the rumble over his head. Like a far away freight train, he thought. Seconds later, there was the ear splitting exploding of the shells. Light flickered briefly over the horizon. Then it was pitch dark until another round of gun fire lit up the night sky.

They began to climb more steeply than before. The trees began to thin out. Then they were in the open.

"Spread out," the word came back. "Keep spread out."

Now Bunty could see men all around him, ahead and on both sides, bent over, moving forward across a meadow. Suddenly firing began on the far side of the hill ahead, making a coughing sound as the shells left their tubes. A star shell burst in the sky, flooding them all in its blinding white glare.

"*Freeze!*"

Bunty stood stock still, trying to look like a tree. But they had been seen. Shells streamed down on them.

"*Hit the dirt!*"

Bunty threw himself face down in the grass. The ground rose on all sides, shaking and exploding. His ears rang with the roaring. Sprays of dirt and steel blew upward all around him. Near him someone cried out in pain. He tried to bury himself in the ground, not daring to reach behind him for his digging tool.

There was a sudden quiet, and the lieutenant yelled: "*Let's go. . . . Let's go! First unit, let's go!*"

The lieutenant was on his feet, running toward the trees on the far side of the field, and Bunty leaped up and followed. Everyone who could was running.

More shells burst, and they threw themselves down. When the screaming of shells stopped, they were on their feet again, moving forward. Bunty rushed past a man on the ground clutching his arm, moaning.

Bunty couldn't stop. He made the last twenty yards to the protection of the trees. Others fell on top of him. The lieutenant raced up. "Spread out! Spread out!" he shouted. "Move! One shell gets the whole bunch of you!"

They struggled apart and raced farther into the trees. Shells were still falling behind them, churning up the torn ground. Their own guns were trying to zero in on the enemy. Ahead of Bunty a man fell, and Bunty helped him up and dragged him along.

The trees thinned toward the top of the hill. They could see the outline of buildings and the steeple of a church against the sky.

"Get the range on that steeple!" the lieutenant shouted. "That's where they're spotting us."

Minutes later, shells began to fall near it, and then there was a direct hit. The steeple exploded in a flash of red flame and bursting timbers.

"Fix bayonets," the lieutenant ordered.

Bunty attached his bayonet to his rifle barrel. Around him, he could hear the clang of steel against steel.

"Keep low!" the sergeant ordered.

They started forward. Meeps began to sing quietly: "*Ven der Fuehrer says ve own der vorld, ve heil!*" Others took up the song, and they began charging up the hill, singing louder and louder. "*Ve heil! Heil! Right in der Fuehrer's face. . . . Heil! Heil!*"

Suddenly, from up ahead, German machine guns began to fire. White flashes appeared at the top of the ridge. Men fell, but the rest charged forward. Bunty pulled the pin of a grenade, and threw it like a forward pass over the ridge and into the teeth of the machine gun. It burst with a roar and a flash of white hot steel.

Two Germans, guns spitting, stood up directly ahead of Bunty. He leveled his M-1 and fired. The Germans fell backward into their fox hole.

Pom . . . pom . . . pom! Guns spoke as they rushed forward. A German leaped toward Meeps, and Meeps' bayonet drove into his chest.

Germans were retreating. The GIs charged forward, bayoneting the enemy before they could climb out of their fox holes. They were in the town now, throwing grenades through windows, waiting for them to explode, then crashing through the door, guns firing. Machine gun and rifle bullets cut through floors and closets. Nazi armored trucks, trying to get away, were blown to bits. And the fighting went on until the town was secured.

As dawn came over the town, men sagged in doorways or on curbs, rifles still at the ready. Bunty saw men from his unit and from the white units side by side. Nobody worried about color here.

They sat down where they were, talking, letting loose.

"Man," Meeps said, mopping his brow, "I don't remember a thing from the time those first shells came flying in! I just kept going."

"Me, too," Bunty said.

"Your first time under fire?" a white GI asked through a mouth filled with processed eggs.

"It sure was," Bunty said.

"You got a good send-off." The guy grinned. "We had the fireworks out for you! Welcome to the club!"

Bunty's unit sergeant came winding his way through them. "Keep your eyes open for any stray Germans," he warned.

Bunty sipped his coffee. A group of Germans, hands raised above their heads, was herded down the street toward the rear.

The sergeant came trotting back. "You'll have to sleep riding today. The trucks are on their way up now."

Men groaned. Units formed up. The trucks came rumbling down the street, and they climbed in. Almost before they started, Bunty had curled up in a corner and was asleep.

They moved ahead slowly, stopping and starting. At noon they pulled into a grove and the kitchen truck rolled up. Every man had a cup of hot coffee and a Spam sandwich. Then they moved slowly on again. They had only made 12 miles by evening.

The trucks halted in a small town that was mostly piles of broken brick. The lieutenant called the unit together near one of the few standing houses.

"Okay, you guys," he said quietly. "We are buttoning up here for the night. First watch is to stay back inside the room so you can't be seen. Report to me immediately if you spot any movement out there. If you are sure it's Jerries attacking, open fire. Keep your grenades handy. The rest of us will go down to the cellar. Now move out."

They moved silently through the house and down into the cellar. It smelled of wet dirt and crumbled plaster and rotten potatoes, but it was a little warmer than the cold night air outside. The sergeant produced a candle and lit it, dropping wax onto the top of his helmet and setting the candle in it. He put his helmet in the middle of the floor, and began heating water over the flame to make himself a cup of coffee.

Bunty dropped off his pack and sat with his back against the wall, his field jacket pulled tight around him.

"Keep your voices down to a whisper," the sergeant said. "We are in Hitler's back pocket, and if there are any Krauts around out there, we don't want to let them know where we are."

"Seems to me we put a big tear in Hitler's pocket last night," Parker whispered.

The sergeant grinned. "We shook them up some," he said. "They weren't expecting us to take that bridge and get across. Right now they are scattered, but they will get together again and hit us with everything they've got. They'd like to shove us back over the river.

"Let them try it," Bunty muttered.

"They will," the sergeant said. "Okay. Bed down, now. Get some sleep."

Bunty moved into a little more comfortable position. He came awake at every sound, and from the shifting and grunts of the men around him, he knew he wasn't the only one having trouble sleeping. There was a strange, waiting quality about the darkness—the feeling of not knowing what was going on outside. Then someone was shaking him. He woke up with a start, grabbing for his rifle.

"Hey, man, what you doing?" Meeps said softly. "Come on. We got guard duty for the rest of the night."

Bunty stumbled to his feet, trying to be quiet. Stiff and cramped, he felt his way up the stairs to the street level. It was colder here, and he shook himself, trying to get some blood going.

Two figures were beside the back window, taking turns peering out into the darkness. "Am I glad to see you," one of the men whispered. "I darn near froze my tail off."

The men whose places they were taking creaked off

to the cellar. Bunty and Meeps took their positions on opposite sides of the window. Bunty checked quietly to be sure his rifle was ready.

The wind whistled in through the shattered window. There was no moon. Bunty strained to see through the darkness. Far to the east he could hear rumbles and see the red flashes of gun fire. He breathed through his mouth so the sound of his own breathing wouldn't clog his ears.

"Man," Meeps whispered. "This is the longest night I ever spent."

The minutes dragged past. It seemed to Bunty he had stood there for hours. Suddenly his attention fastened on something or someone in the yard. He bent down, peering at the shadow. It didn't move. He glanced toward Meeps, but Meeps was staring in another direction.

Bunty turned back to the yard. The shadow was gone. He brought his rifle up slowly to the level of the window sill, expecting any minute to hear the crash of gun fire from outside. He saw another shadow, and then another a little farther to the left. His finger tightened on the trigger. Sweat beaded on his forehead.

Then suddenly his breath let out in a long sigh. He realized what had happened—happened so slowly that he hadn't been aware of the change: daylight was coming. Gray shrubs, gray shed, a gray wagon had slowly become visible. They were what he had seen.

The night was over. The enemy attack had not come.

CHAPTER 9

"Meeps!"

Bunty eased the rifle down, and he and Meeps looked at each other. Grins spread slowly over their faces.

"I was about to shoot me a fence post," Meeps said.

"I had my sights on the shed."

Behind their position, Bunty heard the rumbling of tank engines, like some great iron beasts waking from sleep. The sound of trucks coming into the town grew louder. The sergeant appeared from the cellar, his rifle over his shoulder. "Everything okay?"

"Okay."

"Stay here while I take a look."

The sergeant went through the house and into the street. He was back in a few minutes. "No trouble," he said. "Go wake up the others. Bring your mess kits and fall out for chow."

"*Hot* chow?" Meeps demanded, and the sergeant

nodded. With a yell, Meeps took off for the cellar. "Come and get it! Come and get it!"

The men rushed up out of the cellar, breaking out their mess kits as they came. Down the street, company trucks were drawn up in front of a house, away from German observation. The cooks had been at work. There were fried Spam and pancakes with butter and syrup, two eggs any style, all the coffee the men wanted.

K-rations for two days were handed out. The supply sergeant came along. "Anybody need foot powder? Extra socks?"

One of the white privates Bunty had talked to the night before came over. "Hear another regiment moved through us last night," he said. "They say Jerry is falling back as fast as he can run."

Others joined the talk. . . . *I hear we will break out of this spot and roll into Germany on the double. . . . I hear the 9th Army has crossed at Dusseldorf. . . . Our Looey says he thinks we are the south end of a movement to try and cut off the Ruhr. . . . Man, you know what that means? There will be fighting in front of us and on the left once we get moving.*

Bunty's unit sergeant came toward them. "Okay," he said. "Saddle up and get ready to move out."

They moved into columns. It was full daylight now. They could see the high gray hills of the Rhineland, and in the distance a castle on the Rhine. At 0800 they loaded up. Bunty sat with his rifle between his knees.

They moved slowly down the road. Around them the fields were bare and brown, waiting for spring. Only the pines on the slopes were green. The smell of death, which had hung heavy in the low country, was absent here. Then it struck Bunty suddenly: death had not come here yet. They were in the advance lines.

Progress was slow. Sometimes they rushed ahead for a mile or two, then stopped and waited, or crawled slowly forward. The word came back down the line: *"Road block . . . Road block. . . ."*

They could hear firing, and the whine of shells shrilled toward them.

The order: *"Hit the dirt!"*

Men scrambled from the trucks, clutching their rifles, and threw themselves into the ditches beside the road. Four shells crashed into the field just past them, sending up sprays of black dirt. Then the firing died down. The soldiers ahead of them had cleared out the enemy.

They inched along again. In the late afternoon they rolled into a small village. The trucks pulled to a halt. The sergeant jumped down and went forward for orders. He was back in a few minutes.

"All out!" he cried. "We will secure houses here for the night."

They spread out, ducking from doorway to doorway, checking buildings, alert for any sign of enemy activity. The village was quiet.

They settled into the houses. Bunty and Meeps staked

out an upstairs bedroom for themselves. A shell had gone through one wall and out the other, leaving a huge hole. There was no glass in the window. But there was a large feather bed at one side of the room.

"Look at that!" Meeps said.

Bunty flopped down on the bed with a big sigh. "Bring on the dancing girls," he said.

The sergeant clumped up the stairs. "Okay," he said. "We got a little work to do. Come on."

"I knew it was too good to last," Meeps moaned, as they trailed after the sergeant.

First and second units were assembled in the front room, and the sergeant snapped out the orders: "First unit will camp in the barn. Knock a firing slot in the wall if you have to. If we are attacked, four men from each unit will move to the ditch by the dirt road and spread out. Take a field phone with you to the barn. Keep in touch all night—every five minutes. Okay, spread out now and look sharp!"

One by one, they slipped out of the house and ran along the ditch. Men put up wire for the field telephone as they went. Crawling out of the ditch, they ran to the cover of a small shed. Nothing happened. They advanced to the barn.

The door creaked as they opened it. There was a sudden noise and they froze. "Keep down!" Bunty whispered.

Rifles at the ready, they inched inside, straining to see through the darkness. The sound came again.

"Come out!" Bunty shouted, and then tried to say it in German. Nobody came out.

The sound came again, and Bunty felt the hair at the back of his neck bristling. Nobody had briefed them on a German weapon that made a sound like that.

"*Surrender!*" he shouted. There was no answer.

Meeps made a sudden dive, and then he was snaking up the ladder to the hay loft. A great clucking and fluttering of wings filled the air. Dust flew, and white chickens suddenly scattered in all directions.

"Get one!" Meeps yelled from the hay loft, and every GI made a dive for a bird. Meeps tumbled out of the hay loft, a chicken in each hand. Bunty chased a fat hen into a corner and managed to capture her. Other GIs came back, chickens in hand. All together they had caught six birds.

"Are we going to eat tonight!" Meeps cried, hopping about with an angry chicken in each hand. "We got us a first-class supper."

While two men stood watch to cover their position, the others plucked and cleaned the chickens. Meeps ordered a fire pit dug in the middle of the dirt floor.

"Hope we don't burn the place down," he said, and put a couple of chickens on a green wood stick to set them to roasting.

"Don't forget to call the sergeant every five minutes!" Parker warned. "We don't want extra company here—not right now."

Bunty made the call. The chickens were roasted, two by two, the men sitting happily around the glowing coals of the fire pit. Even when everyone had eaten all he could hold, there was still chicken left.

"How about taking what's left to the men at the machine gun position?" Bunty asked.

"Right!" Meeps said and, snatching off his helmet, he packed the left-over chicken in it. Bunty took it and, ducking out of the barn, worked his way to the stone wall where the men were. "P-s-s-s-t!" he whispered.

A rifle leveled at him, and a sharp voice snapped: "What's the pass word?"

For an awful second Bunty's mind went blank, and then he quickly said: *"Texas Rangers!"*

"Advance and show yourself!"

Bunty crawled forward, the tin hat full of roast chicken in his hands. "Private George Bunty," he gulped.

"What are you doing here?" the voice whispered.

"I brought some chicken." Bunty passed the hat up.

Somebody took it. There were whispers and quick movements. Then someone said: "Thanks, pal! Now get moving before the sergeant finds out what's going on!"

Grinning, Bunty made his way back to the barn. He took his turn standing watch, and then curled up in the hay. It was the warmest he had been for a long time, and he slept like a baby. When the gun fire came a little before dawn, he just dug deeper into the hay.

That night gave the men the feeling that the Nazis were all on the run. When they trucked out in the morning, they were in high spirits.

"Hey, Jerries!" Meeps yelled, sticking his head over the side of the truck. "Pull in your swastikas! We are coming to get you!"

"Knock it off," the sergeant growled. "You guys are still green. You think the war's over because nobody got shot up last night."

"Us Black Timber Wolves get going, nobody's going to stop us!" Meeps yelled back.

Bunty saw the white units in the truck ahead of him, and he remembered the way they had mingled along the slow miles they had traveled. They *were* the Black Timber Wolves—part of the 104th. And if the Big Brass hemmed them in, the fighting men didn't seem to care what color their skin was. They were just soldiers.

Toward dusk they came into hilly country with a stand of trees by the road. They pulled off into it and buttoned down for the night. It seemed like the beginning of nowhere. There didn't seem to be any reason to stop here, or anything to worry about up ahead.

They settled down in the hollows and ate, then tried to curl up tight to keep warm. They didn't sleep much —it was too cold, and the rain that had started to fall turned to sleet. Toward morning they woke up stiff, cramped, complaining—wishing they would move out.

The lieutenant came through, warning them that there

might be action, and the sergeants were prowling like nervous dogs. *"Okay . . . keep it quiet. . . . Word is the Jerries are dug in near here. Stay alert."*

Bunty's feet seemed to be slowly freezing in his wet boots. And all he could see was the sky getting grayer. Off in the distance, he could hear the *boom-boom* of guns, but it was too far away to worry about.

Before dawn they were ordered out, and they trucked along to another area in the woods. The sergeant ordered them out in the rain, and they moved through the trees. It did not feel real to Bunty. It was quiet—too quiet. There wasn't even any shell fire in the distance. But out there ahead of them some place was the enemy.

They started forward, bending low, running. They went down a hill and up the other side. Then ahead of them was a meadow, and beyond it a hilly rise with a few trees on it. That was where the Germans had their front line. Bunty thought, this is going to be tough.

The order came, and the men charged forward. They were hit by heavy machine gun fire right in the middle of their advance, and it stopped them cold. German bullets swept across the meadow like a giant mowing machine, cutting them down. Bunty hit the dirt.

"We need guns on the ridge," the lieutenant shouted into the field telephone. Moments later the screaming thunder of .155's began landing on Nazi pill boxes.

The heavy gun fire was followed by smoke shells. Bunty saw the white curves spouting up like Fourth of

July fireworks. Smoke drifted forward, and gradually the whole Nazi line was buried in a whirling gray wall.

Bunty's unit had been shattered. New men came up from the rear. A team from company headquarters rushed up with a satchel charge of TNT to shove into the pill box—if the men with the rifles could pin the Germans down long enough for them to get it there.

"Come on!" Bunty grunted, urging himself and his unit forward. They moved into the smoke, brown uniforms nearly lost against the dirty color of the hills.

Bunty could hear the noise of small arms and now and then the sound of a grenade as the end units tried to surround the Germans. The chatter of guns rose so high that it set his teeth on edge. His unit was pinned down, and the men lay there. Night came, and they tried to move, but the Germans zeroed in on them.

Dawn came up. Right and left of Bunty, men lay dead. And then the order came. Bunty threw himself forward with the others, giving everything he had, trying to knock out the pill box and the connecting trenches.

A breeze rose, and the smoke screen blew away. Bunty could see men in little lumps across the field, with a few men at the far edges of the opening taking what cover they could find from the bullets. Bunty threw himself down behind a tree. Bullets tore off the bark.

Orders were coming fast from the rear: *"Move out! Move out! We've got to take that pill box!"* The captain's messenger came forward, bending over, trying to keep from being hit. "Captain's orders," he gasped. "We've got to knock out that pill box!"

Bunty inched forward, firing at the slits of the pill box, trying to keep the enemy busy while the other men worked their way up. A spray of return fire chewed at him, and he rolled, praying.

Soldiers snaked nearer to the pill box, the satchel of TNT passing from hand to hand quickly, each man wanting to get rid of it before it was smacked by a bullet. German fire pinned them down, and they froze. Then they wormed their way forward again—the line thinning out as men were hit.

Bunty inched ahead. His finger felt stiff from firing round after round. Now he was only yards away from the pill box, but off to one side. Ahead of him, men were still trying to move the TNT satchel forward. Four were dead. One was wounded. The others tried to blast their way forward. A line of Nazi fire cut them down. The satchel lay on the slope.

Bunty saw it, and tried to edge his way toward it, but a blast of enemy fire pinned him down. The sergeant shouted at him: "Keep your fire on the pill box. We will get someone through if you do your job!"

Bunty threw himself to the ground. Someone shouted: "Give the men a chance! Keep them busy! Keep firing!"

Bunty kept firing. Sweat ran down into his eyes, and he wiped it away. The satchel lay there on the side of the hill under German fire. Suddenly a man was run-

ning, bent over, clawing forward. He was a little guy, and his ears stuck out from his head.

"Meeps!" Bunty cried, and his rifle blasted at the enemy pill box.

Meeps rushed ahead. Muscles strained in his legs as he churned up the slope. His hands gripped the satchel, one arm hooked through the strap, and he threw himself forward. His body hit concrete—he had made it! He dropped his rifle and raised the satchel in one hand. Bunty's rifle spat at the pill box, trying to cover him.

Meeps tried to push the satchel into the pill box. From inside, Germans struggled to push it back. Bullets slammed down at Meeps, into his back, his legs, his body. With his remaining strength, he pushed the canvas bag into the pill box. Smoke rose out of the pill box as it exploded. The blast slammed Bunty to the ground, and gray smoke curled toward him. He shoved himself up, tears running down his face.

"Meeps," he yelled. "Meeps!"

CHAPTER 10

Clean-up Missions

The next day, new men came up from the rear to take the places of the dead. Bunty felt old and tired. In his mind he saw Meeps' body, the way it had twisted those last seconds. He saw Meeps' hands pressing the TNT satchel down to explode on the enemy. . . .

The chaplain—a minister in army uniform—edged his way up beside Bunty. "Rough going?" he asked.

Bunty didn't answer. The chaplain sat down, leaning forward, his elbows on his knees. "There isn't any answer," he said quietly. "Nobody knows why it has to be one man instead of another. Nobody knows."

"He didn't have to be in the fighting unit," Bunty said tightly.

"Because he was a Negro?" the chaplain asked. "Do you think he would rather have been in a service unit? Is that what Meeps wanted?"

"No," Bunty muttered. "He wanted in."

"And he was," the chaplain said. "He was a good soldier."

For the next two days they met little enemy resistance. They got to their next stopping point at dusk of the third night. In a field on the right there was firing. Beyond, smoke stacks rose black against the gray sky.

The unit leader came up to them. "All right, men, we are moving out. No smoking. No noise."

Bunty fixed the straps on his pack and shouldered his weapon. Two scouts moved out ahead of them, and then the unit leader. After him the men marched along, five paces apart.

They reached a grove of trees. It was almost completely dark now, and the columns began to close up to keep contact with each other.

At the far edge of the grove, the lieutenant motioned them to get down and spread out. Ahead of them was a field full of ditches, clumps of bushes along their sides. They could see the factory looming in the darkness, lighted now and then by the flash of exploding shells.

There was a popping sound, and Bunty froze against the ground. High in the air there was a blinding light, bathing the field in white glare. The men halted. Bunty waited for the chatter of machine guns, but there was only the boom of their own shells falling on the factory and on the slope and village beyond.

The light faded, and Bunty blinked his eyes, getting them used to the darkness again. The unit leader was moving forward slowly across the field, bending low. The rest of the men got up and followed, rifles ready. The field was a sea of mud, and their boots made a sucking sound as they walked.

They were 50 feet from the factory. The lieutenant broke into a run, firing, and the men followed. Bunty saw some Germans trying to get their gun into action in a window. He pulled the pin on a grenade and threw it. It exploded, leaving a hole where the window had been.

They rushed up to the entrance and swarmed through doors and windows. Inside they took cover behind machinery and pillars, firing at the flash of German guns, tossing grenades, blasting a roar of sound and steel across the floor. From the shelter of a huge machine, Bunty glimpsed German soldiers on a steel cat walk, trying to get into position. He fired. Bullets slammed into the floor near him. Beside him a gun roared back.

Dodging his way past machinery, Bunty found himself at the top of a flight of steps leading down into even greater darkness. He started down, and a stream of bullets from below blazed up the stairs. He dodged back and sent down a grenade. Fire seared up and steel fragments hit against the walls. He rushed down into the sharp smell of gun powder and hot steel. It was pitch black.

He dropped flat on the floor, spraying bullets around him.

"*Kamerad!*" a voice called.

"*Komm raus—hände hoch!*" Bunty shouted back in German. "Come out—hands up!" In the gloom of the basement he heard someone moving forward, and he inched back toward the stair well, where some light came in. Keeping out of sight, he waited. The sound stopped. Bunty could see no one.

Suddenly a GI rushed down the stairs. "Look out!" Bunty yelled. The GI threw himself forward. A machine gun hammered bullets against the stair well. Bunty aimed at the glow of the gun flash and fired. Two shots banged out and then his rifle was empty. He rolled to another position and loaded again. The other GI was firing. The machine gun answered. Bunty aimed low and squeezed off another burst of shots. The machine gun stopped firing. More GIs were coming down the steps.

"I think I got him!" Bunty yelled.

"Are there any more?"

"Don't think so."

They pushed through the darkness, but the cellar was cleaned out, and they went back upstairs. Fires were burning. A stray bullet bounced off the machinery, but the remains of the German unit seemed to have retreated. Bunty found his own group bent low beside the windows, waiting for an attack.

The sergeant came up to them, ducking low to keep

from being outlined against the windows. "Who's on watch?"

"Parker and Allen."

The sergeant ducked away again. Bunty opened his K-ration and chewed on the hard chocolate bar. In a few minutes the sergeant was back. "B Company is moving past us to take the town," he said. "Don't fire at anyone unless you are sure it's a German." He moved off to warn the men on watch.

Shells began to crash into the town. Outside, figures moved past the factory and up the hill. German guns screamed, their shells bursting in showers of flame and steel.

A soldier came rushing forward. "The lieutenant says to fire at the ridge line and give B Company some cover!"

Bunty looked for the flicker of white light that meant a German machine gun pill box and fired. From the balcony, guns opened up. A grenade blossomed on the side of the hill. The rain of fire continued, keeping the Germans pinned down so that B Company could get closer. From the back of the factory, American guns opened up. The German guns stopped suddenly.

The lieutenant ran up. "Cease fire! Cease fire!"

The slamming of the grenades died out. Bunty could hear small arms' fire on the ridge, and then there was a great burst of firing. They could tell by the sound that it was American. The Germans were pulling back.

They buttoned up the town that night, and for the best part of a week they met little enemy resistance. The weather was warmer, fresh green growth began to cover over the scars of war.

They were on a clean-up mission now, combing the villages that the armor had passed through—and Germans had moved back into. Sometimes the fighting was fierce, but more often as the Americans moved in, the Germans came out with their hands up.

Deep into the northwest part of Germany they went. Past Paderborn they turned east, meeting with elements of the Ninth Army that had come down from the north, sealing the Germans in the Ruhr pocket. East of Berlin, the Russians were moving toward that city.

They were bouncing along a road one sunny day when

the trucks stopped suddenly and the cry: *"Germans ahead!"* went from front to rear.

"Down! Down!"

They climbed down and moved into the fields, taking cover behind rocks and bushes. A jeep roared up beside the lead truck.

"There's a bunch of Germans in the town ahead," he said. "We want to get them to surrender instead of fight. We need your men to surround the village and bottle them up."

"Get ready to move out!" the order came.

A row of tanks moved up. The men clawed their way onto them, helping each other up to the rear deck. Bunty got a place on the lead tank, and they roared off down the road and across the field.

The tank commander of Bunty's machine rode with the top open and his head and shoulders sticking out so he could pass on information to the driver. The radio in the tank kept up a constant stream of orders and messages from other units and from headquarters.

The tanks rolled over bushes and small trees with the rifle men ducking the branches and trying to hold on. They could see the town up ahead, and other tanks spreading out to block all roads.

"Able Leader to Able One!" the radio called. "Do you read me?"

"Able Leader, this is Able One. Read you loud and clear."

"Proceed to six four zero at three zero zero. Stand fast and button up. Do you read me?"

"Roger."

"Over and out."

The tank ground over the highway and started down the bank on the other side. A bullet hit the hatch and whined away.

"It's from the village," the tank commander said. He dropped lower in the tank. "Able Two, Three, and Four, come in! Fire coming from the left flank. Can you spot him?"

Another bullet hit, burying itself in one of the food boxes tied to the top of the tank. Bunty saw a puff of smoke from a window in one of the village barns. His rifle slammed twice, then again. Another of the German's shots hit the tank.

"You got him spotted?" the commander yelled.

"Left window of that barn on the edge of town. Building nearest us."

Bunty fired at the window. Other men joined in.

"Stand clear!" the commander ordered. Slowly the tank began to turn toward the barn, its cannon lowering. Men scrambled around, trying to find safer positions.

Suddenly the tank stopped. The cannon roared, and it nearly knocked Bunty loose from his hold. His ears rang from the blast. The cannon spoke again. And there, where the German had been, was a huge hole. Smoke began pouring out.

The tank moved ahead again and into position on the east road. The commander radioed back that they were buttoned up as ordered.

"Stay put," came the order.

The men climbed down from the tank and got in attack position. But then along the edge of the town, white flags began to appear. The Germans had decided to surrender without more fighting.

CHAPTER 11

V-E Day

Two days later, on April 13, as they moved in west of the Harz mountains, the news spread through the ranks.

President Roosevelt is dead. . . . FDR . . . the Commander in Chief! It did not seem possible. Men looked at each other blankly, feeling a personal loss.

"He should have lived to see the end of the war. We would have brought him a victory in a few more weeks," Bunty thought.

The men were silent as they moved out on a highway. There was little resistance along the way. White flags fluttered from windows along the main streets of towns and from the front yards of farm houses. From the east, the thunder of Russian guns could be heard. German soldiers by the hundreds were surrendering.

They rumbled into Sandersdorf late in April, and suddenly they met sharp resistance. German fire blocked a cross road. A GI fell trying to cross the street, and another ran out, dragging him to safety behind a wall.

"Clean them out!" the sergeant ordered.

Ducking and dodging, they worked their way up the street. A German tank rounded a corner, spitting fire, but an advancing American tank blasted it to smoking ruin. Enemy fire seemed to be coming from all directions. Bunty tossed a grenade through a shattered window, but it was thrown back into the street, and he dove for cover as it exploded.

GIs blasted through the doors of buildings and fired round after round through the ceilings into rooms above. One by one they began to round up the enemy. Bunty could hardly believe his eyes. They were frightened kids— fourteen, fifteen years old. They had held the block for an hour against his unit. Bunty hated to think how many were dead.

"It doesn't make you feel good to have to fight kids," he thought, as he helped get them into trucks that would take them to PW cages.

The shout came from back along the street. "Enemy attack! Enemy attack!"

He dived for the door of a house and raced up to the second floor. Coming toward him he saw the column of Germans. He raised his rifle. His eye caught a flicker of movement across the street and he swung around,

firing, just as a German raised his arm to throw a grenade. The German fell forward and lay still in the street.

Machine gun bullets smacked against the side of the house. Two Germans ran forward, trying to set up a machine gun in the mouth of an alley. Bunty got one of them. The other picked up the gun and ran back out of sight.

GIs were firing from almost every house. The Germans had taken cover. Bunty kept his fire on the mouth of the alley so the gun couldn't be set up.

The sergeant came racing in. "Tanks are moving up to help us. Get out and stay even with them."

The tanks rumbled next to the house and Bunty and the others dodged into position. They moved forward, beating back the resistance, clearing out snipers, knocking out the few remaining machine guns. The enemy began to surrender and come in. Old men, boys in their early teens, soldiers who had seen long months of duty and the dream of conquering the world end in defeat.

It was near the end of April when they got into Bitterfeld. A few miles away across the Elbe River were the Russian forces and, in between, 20,000 German troops gave up the defense of the Fatherland.

Planes dropped notices directing the enemy soldiers to present themselves at the river in groups of 500 every half hour. The engineers threw up foot bridges. Bunty and his unit were assigned patrol duty.

Bunty was on patrol when he got his first sight of the Russian soldiers. They shouted and waved and, with some of the other men, Bunty made his way across the bent strands of bombed-out German bridges to meet them. They couldn't speak each other's language, but there was a lot of back slapping and laughter and souvenir trading. Bunty wished Meeps could be there. There was nothing he had liked better than a good trade.

And then, at 0940 on the seventh of May, Supreme Headquarters of the AEF announced ". . . the German High Command signed the surrender of all German land, sea, and air forces in Europe. . . . All operations will cease. . . ." It was signed "Eisenhower."

Two days later V-E Day was announced to the world. The war in Europe was over.

What next? Would they be sent to the Pacific? They hadn't thought much about the war going on there, but now they did.

"Well, I guess we can learn to fight in the jungles without too much trouble," Bunty said, grinning.

"And every man gets a leave at home before he ships out," Parker said. "Those are Eisenhower's orders."

"I hope we stay with the Timber Wolves," Bunty said. "It's a great outfit."

Then, without warning, the word came: the Negro fighting men were being returned to service units.

It couldn't be true! They had signed up for fighting. They had fought side by side with the white GIs. Nobody had thought about color. It hadn't mattered.

But now the color line was back. And the men realized that no matter how well they had fought, the old idea still held: the Negro's place was in service units.

On the twenty-seventh of May, a special ceremony was held for the Negroes. Brigadier General Benjamin O. Davis spoke to them. "You have proved that white and Negro troops can serve—and fight—side by side. You have won the respect of your comrades." Major General

Terry Allen praised their brave service. The division commander decorated two men with the Silver Star and ten with the Bronze Star.

But the praise and the honors meant little to the men as they were moved back. Spirits dropped. Word spread that service units of the Negroes would go directly to the Pacific and would not get the promised leaves.

Men felt that everything they had fought for had been smashed. Bunty thought that trouble would be coming—bad trouble—unless something was done.

He sat one night in July talking to Parker and some of the others. "It's no good trying to raise the men's spirits," Bunty said. "Talk won't do any good. It's going to take some kind of action to do it."

They made up a plan that night. Four of them would go AWOL and try to get to headquarters in Frankfurt to see General Eisenhower.

They drew straws to see who would go. Bunty was disappointed to find that he had drawn a short straw. So had Parker. The four others would go.

They slipped away that night. In camp Bunty and Parker waited, wondering if the men got to Frankfurt; if Eisenhower would see them?

"One wrong thing happens and this whole place goes up like a powder keg," Bunty said.

Then the men came back, riding in an official car, grins on their faces.

They had not seen Eisenhower—he hadn't been in Frankfurt. But they had seen his military assistant.

"He took us to dinner in the headquarters mess hall," one of the men said. "We were the first Negroes ever in that dining room."

"But what happened?" Bunty said.

"On Monday we saw General Paul. And here's what he told us: all Negro fighting men will be sent through the United States to the Pacific. We are still combat troops. We do get our leaves."

The news was announced to the men. Excitement flew through the camp. Men talked of nothing but having their leaves and getting on to the Pacific.

"They've got camps set up already here in Europe, training for jungle war. We will be heading for one soon."

But it didn't work out that way after all. Less than a month later, on August 14, the Pacific war ended.

Days later they joined an all-Negro regiment. New clothing was issued. Thoughts turned toward home.

And on a sunny day early the next month, ship-out orders came. Trucks took them to the port. Carrying their heavy bags, they moved along the pier and up the gang plank onto the transport ship. Late in the afternoon, they set sail for home.

So many months ago they had crossed the Atlantic, guarded by other ships, fearful of attack. Now they sailed in peace. Behind them they left many of their comrades, black and white, their graves marked by crosses.

Bunty stood at the rail watching as the ship came into New York harbor, and he saw the Statue of Liberty. As they came to the pier, a crowd of friends and families were cheering and waving, and a great feeling of pride for the Negro soldiers went through Bunty.

They were good soldiers—good men—and they had fought and worked and put their lives on the line like every other GI. They had written a record for the whole world to read, and it spoke of more than war.

Bunty thought about Meeps—the little guy with big ears and a heart full of courage.

"We proved it, didn't we, Meeps?" he said to himself. "Maybe some day it will count."

And he saw Meeps' grin, and heard his answer: "We proved it, man! And it will count!"

J33